一本就能

Hold住工作、享受生活的
情境英語
Email寫作書
附超值便利貼光碟，輕鬆寫信！

還在糾結英語Email該怎麼寫？
How to write Email in English?

How to use...信件抬頭？ How to write...個人要求？
How to request...對方回信？ How to end...信末祝福語？

信箱Email太多沒時間回嗎？有了這本，就能迅速回完這些信：
【留學申請】、【求職面試】、【業務採購】、【公關客服】、【社交邀請】、【旅遊訂房訂票】
全都適用！

便利貼光碟

本書有三寶：
大寶：實用！專業英語老師親自傳授英語書信的撰寫眉角！
二寶：齊全！囊括36個工作與生活上的情境，教你信件往返應付自如！
小寶：方便！隨書附贈超值模版便利「貼」光碟，讓你輕鬆Copy and Paste！

編者序

　　除了社交軟體，Email也是工作、生活上不可或缺的一項工具，無論時區相差多久，空間距離相隔多遠，只要透過網路發送，訊息的傳遞並沒有什麼太大的困難。但是用英文寫Email對很多人來說，因為不知道該如何下筆，反而是一大夢魘。

　　本書舉了36個工作、學校、生活上會遇到的情境為例，提供寫作策略、信件大綱，與專業英文老師撰寫的範本，讓讀者方便參考、琢磨。另附模版便利貼光碟，讓讀者能於Email寫信上更得心應手。

編輯部

CONTENTS 目次

主題 **1** 求學求職大小事！

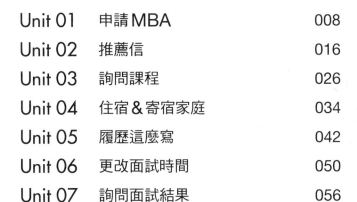

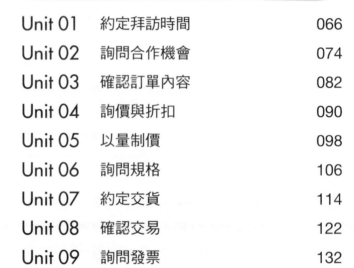

主題 4　愛旅遊，玩社交！

主題1　求學求職大小事！

Unit
01

申請MBA

寫作策略

 Who are you writing to? 寫給誰？

Evan Wang

Step 2 **What** do you want to know about? 你想知道什麼？

Eligibility requirements and number of participants
Language of Instruction
Duration of the program
Fees and Expenses
Course Credits
Living arrangements

Outline 這樣擬

寫信目的	開場先感謝對方協助申請留學，註明學校等基本資訊。
詢問細節	詢問留學資訊。
敬請回覆	要求對方收到訊息後回覆。
信　尾	客套語＋署名。

看看老師怎麼寫

Dear Mr. Wang,

Thank you so much for providing information about business schools in the U.S.A. I've read the files for all the top-ranking business schools, and I'm very interested in applying to the one-year full-time MBA programs in University of Southern California. Here are still some questions I'd like to consult you about the above program:

1. How many students typically participate in this program?
2. How many international students study at this school?
3. What are the language requirements for international students?
4. Are language requirements fulfilled while abroad? Or do they provide immersion program on-site?
5. What's the GPA requirement for admission?
6. Is there scholarship or financial aids available for international students?

I would much appreciate if you could reply to the above questions a.s.a.p.

Sincerely,
Jordan Liao

 中文翻譯

王先生您好：

十分感謝您提供美國商學院相關資料。我已經閱讀過所有美國頂尖商學院的資料，我對於申請南加大的MBA課程很感興趣。

以下是我針對此課程的疑問，想諮詢您的意見：

1. 通常研讀這學位的學生有多少人？
2. 該校有多少國際學生？
3. 國際學生的入學英語標準為何？
4. 在就讀前就得先在海外達到英語標準嗎？還是校方有提供國際學生到校後，就讀語言銜接課程？
5. 申請入學的平均學業成績為何？
6. 有提供國際學生獎學金或財務上的協助嗎？

若您能盡速回答以上疑惑，將不勝感激。

Jordan Liao敬上

關鍵單字片語

1. **apply** *vi.* *vt.* 申請；實施 (+to)

   I'm preparing all the academic documents to apply to the law school at Harvard University.

   我正在準備所有學業相關文件以申請哈佛大學法學院。

2. **consult** *vi.* *vt.* 商議；諮詢

   Many international students consult student affairs officers for applying for scholarships.

   很多國際學生會向學生事務處員工詢問如何申請獎學金。

3. **international** *adj.* 國際的

   International students consist of 15% of the total number of students in this school.

   國際學生佔了這所學校學生總數的百分之15。

4. **requirement** *n.* 錄取條件

   What are the GPA and language requirements for admission to the school?

   要入學這所學校的學業成績和語言能力門檻為何？

5. **abroad** *adv.* 在海外；在國外

   Only a few undergraduate students at this school consider applying to study abroad programs.

   這所學校只有少數學生考慮要申請到國外留學的課程。

6. **immersion program** *n.* （為國際學生開的）語言銜接課程

   This school offers great immersion programs and orientations for international students.

   這所學校為國際學生提供很棒的語言銜接課程和新生訓練。

主題 1

給力句型解說 👉

現在完成式 have/has + p.p.

使用時機：

1. 過去開始的動作（但沒有明確的時間），到現在前已經完成。有時會有關鍵字already, just, yet。

   The professor **has already read** our reports, but he **hasn't graded** them **yet**.

   教授已經看過我們的報告，但還沒打成績。

2. 過去開始的動作（但沒有明確的時間），到現在仍在持續中。關鍵字for, since。

   He **has had** a cold **for** more than a week. He **hasn't come** to school **since** last Tuesday.

   他已經感冒超過一個星期了。他從上週二到現在都沒來上學。

3. 從過去到現在累積的經驗或次數。關鍵字once, twice, many times, before, ever。

   A: **Have** you **ever been** to Tokyo Disneyland?

   　你去過東京迪士尼樂園嗎？

   B: Yes, I**'ve been** there **twice**.

   　是的，我去過兩次。

複合形容詞：adj. -現在分詞 / 過去分詞

1. 形容詞-現在分詞 (V-ing)：被形容的名詞當主詞時，動詞用主動語態。

   如：

   a **top-ranking**（排名頂尖的）school → a school which **ranks** top

   wide-ranging（廣泛的）discussions → discussions which **range**

wide

loose-fitting（鬆身的）clothes → clothes which **fit** loose

2. 形容詞-過去分詞（p.p.）：被形容的名詞當主詞時，動詞用被動語態。

如：

a high-priced（索價很高的）designer handbag → a designer handbag which **is priced** high

a low-paid（薪水很低的）job → a job which **is paid** low

換個對象寫寫看

Dear **Ms. Brown**,

I'm very interested in off-site online MBA programs offered in _____University.

Here are still some questions I'd like to consult you about the above program:

1. **Are all courses for this degree offered online?**
2. **How are the online courses delivered?**
3. **How do students interact with the instructor and each other?**
4. **What are the admissions deadlines?**
5. **How many credits are required for a degree?**
6. **Are course grades based on test scores, essays, or both?**

I would much appreciate if you could reply to the above questions a.s.a.p.

Faithfully,
Jenny Huang

Brown小姐您好：

我對於＿＿＿＿＿大學的線上MBA課程很感興趣。

以下是我針對此課程的疑問，想諮詢您的意見：

1. 這個學程的所有課程都是可以線上學習的嗎？

2. 線上課程的上課方式為何？

3. 學生和講師如何互動？

4. 申請截止時間為何？

5. 需要修幾個學分才能取得學位？

6. 學科評分的標準是考試或是報告，亦或兩者皆為評分標準？

如蒙回覆，不勝感激。

Jenny Huang 敬上

 好用句型大補湯

費用部分

I'd like to know how much money I have to prepare for this one year program, including tuition fee, books, housing, meals, special excursions, and a round-way airfare. Since costs are my primary concern, I'was wondering if there were scholarships, financial aid available for international students.

我想要知道這一年的費用大致上我要準備多少。包含學費、書籍費用、住宿、餐飲、校外教學，以及一張來回機票。因為費用是我主要選校考量的指

標，所以我想詢問該校是否提供國際學生獎助學金？

住宿家庭或住宿安排

I'd like to know more about accommodation arrangements. The questions are as follows.

1. How many types of housing arrangements are there to choose from?
2. How far is the housing from the university?
3. Are meals included?
4. Can the program accommodate students with special dietary needs (e.g. food allergies)?

Your kind reply to the above inquires will be highly appreciated.

我想知道更多有關住宿的安排。以下是我的疑問：

1. 有多少種類的住宿可以選擇？
2. 住宿地點距離學校約多近？
3. 有提供伙食嗎？
4. 是否可以照顧有特殊飲食需求的學生（如：食物過敏）？

如蒙回覆，不勝感激。

其他問句

1. Does the school offer postgraduate courses within my major?
   這所學校是否有提供和我目前主修科目相關的碩士課程？
2. I'd like to know how long it takes to graduate. And I'd like to know the classes are offered regularly.
   我想知道修業時間(就讀到畢業會花多久時間)。我也想要知道所有科目是否按時開課。

Unit
02
推薦信

寫作策略

Step **1** **Who** are you writing to? 要寫給誰？

Professor Yang

Step **2** What do you **request**? 你要求什麼？

to write a recommendation letter

Step **3** **What** school/field do you apply to? 你申請什麼學校？

Law School, Princeton University

Step **4** **Why** do you apply to this school/program/course?
為什麼要申請？

interested in the program, it provides a dual degree
program

Step **5** Other **details** 其他細節

admission term, application due

Outline 這樣擬

寒　　喧	開場先向對方問候。
寫信目的	提出請對方寫推薦函的需求，告知要申請學校和科系。
細　　節	分多段寫申請動機、理由，讓教授更了解你的細節。
敬請回覆	要求對方收到訊息後回覆確認。
信　　尾	客套語＋署名。

主題 1

看看老師怎麼寫

Dear Professor Yang,

Happy New Year! I hope you had a great night celebrating and that you are enjoying the time off!

I am writing to ask if you would be willing, time permitting, to write a letter of recommendation for me for my application to law schools. At Boston College, your classes were on my favorites list and hugely contributed to my development and growth as an individual. I wanted to ask you first for a letter because I believe you were familiar with my approach and dedication to academics.

I am currently applying to law schools for admission in September 2016. My top choice is Princeton University. I am particularly interested in doing a dual degree program to also receive an MBA; if I were admitted, I would be applying for the dual degree program during my first year of law school.

Thank you in advance for your time, and consideration. I also wanted to extend an additional thank you for the time I spent under your instruction.

If you are available to write a recommendation letter, please let me know, and I can send you further information. My applications are due by March 22nd.
I look forward to hearing from you, and I wish you a very Happy New Year!

All the best,
Daniel Liao

中文翻譯

楊教授您好：
新年快樂！祝福您今晚很開心的慶祝新年，同時好好享受新年假期。

我寫這封是想詢問您，如果時間允許的話，有沒有意願協助我撰寫申請法學院的推薦信？在波士頓大學求學時，我很喜歡您的課程，您的課程促使我不斷成長。您是我最先詢問的教授，因為我相信您對於我在學業上的讀書方式和努力很熟悉。

我目前正在申請法學院，預計2016年九月入學。我的首選是普林斯頓大學，我對它結合法學與商學管理碩士的雙學位課程很有興趣。若我能錄取，我會在法學院第一學期提出雙學位申請。

在此先謝謝您撥冗閱讀此信。我想藉此機會再次感謝您在我大學期間給我的教導。

請讓我知道您能否撥空幫我撰寫推薦信，若可以的話我會再給您進一步的訊息。我的申請截止日期是3月22日。

期待收到您的消息，祝您新年快樂！

Daniel 廖　敬上

關鍵單字片語

1. **letter of recommendation**　*n.*　推薦信

   Try to get letters of recommendation from bosses and colleagues to highlight the strength of your work experience.

   嘗試向老闆或同事取得推薦信，強調你在工作經驗上的強項。

2. **dedication**　*n.*　供奉；努力 (+ to)

   A party was held to celebrate the retired worker's dedication to the company.

   為了感謝這名退休員工對公司付出的心力，公司辦了一場派對。

   dedicate　*vt.*　以……奉獻

3. **academic**　*n.*　學業；學術

   Most people in Asian countries put a lot of emphasis on academics.

   大多數亞洲人重視課業。

   academic　*adj.*　學術的；學校的

4. **admission**　*n.*　入學

   The admission committee evaluates each candidate's academic

background.

入學委員會評估每位申請人的學術背景。

admit   *vi.*   *vt.*   承認；准許進入

5. dual degree program雙學位

A dual degree program involves a student's working for two different university degrees in parallel.

雙學位是指一位學生同時唸兩個不同的學位。

6. instruction   *n.*   指導

Install the machine according to the manufacturer's instructions.

請根據製作商的指示安裝這台機器。

給力句型解說

be willing to V 願意去做……

The alumni of the school is willing to donate money to the school to help build a lab.

這位校友願意捐助資金給校方蓋一座實驗室。

延伸片語：

1. **be reluctant to V**: 猶豫，不太願意去做……

   The child is reluctant to talk about how he was bullied.

   這個小孩不願意講他被霸凌的經過。

2. **be eager/keen to V**: 急著，迫切的想去做……

   Everyone is eager to know the result of the relay.

   每個人都急著想知道大隊接力的結果。

3. **would rather VR₁ than VR₂**: 寧願做VR₁也不願做VR₂

These revolutionists would rather die than yield to tyranny.

這些革命人士寧願死也不願屈服於暴政。

獨立分詞構句 S₁ + V₁-ing/V1-pp..., S₂ + V₂...

time permitting 如果時間允許的話

S₁ + V₁-ing/V₁-pp..., S₂ + V₂...（或前後互換）

省略連接詞，動詞變分詞：主動 → ing、被動 → p.p.（S₁與S₂主詞不同）

1. If time (S₁) **permits**, we (S₂) will stop off in Hong Kong to do some shopping.

   → Time **permitting**, we will stop off in Hong Kong to do some shopping.

   （刪除附屬連接詞if，連接句子的主動語態動詞permits要變現在分詞 permitting。）

   若時間允許的話，我們可以過境香港去購物。

2. There (S₁) were fireworks of all sorts, and each (S₂) **was** brightly **colored**.

   → There were fireworks of all sorts, each **being** brightly colored.

   → There were fireworks of all sorts, each brightly **colored**.

   這裡有不同種類的煙火，每一種都被塗上鮮豔的色彩。

Dear **Mr. Wang,**

I am writing to ask if you could, time-permitting, write a recommendation letter for my application to MBA in Princeton University for September 2017. The more I learned about business management in this company, the more I became convinced that pursuing a degree in MBA would be a good path for me.

I asked you to write this letter because of the respect I have for your work and opinions. As my supervisor, you would be able to write about my analytical, problem-solving and communication skills, as well as my ability to provide high quality service to diverse, global clients, handle heavy workloads, and my potential to be successful in business school and beyond.

I know this is going to be a busy month at work, so I understand if it won't be possible to do this - either way, I appreciate your help!

Thank you very much for your help.

Best regards,
Christine Chen

王先生您好：

我寫信是想詢問，您是否可以，若時間允許的話，幫我寫推薦信，以便我申請**2017**年秋季入學的普林斯頓大學企管碩士課程。隨著我在這間公司工作期間越來越了解商業管理，我就越確信追求**MBA**學位是很適合我的途徑。

之所以想請您寫這封推薦信，主要是我十分敬重您的工作專業和意見。身為我的主管，我相信您可以著墨於我的分析與解決問題的能力，還有我能為不同類型全球各地的客戶提供高品質服務的能力，而且我能應付高工作量，有潛力能在商學院和之後的工作有所成就。

我知道接下來這個月很忙，若您不能撥空撰寫推薦信，我完全能理解。不論如何，我都謝謝您的幫忙。

Christine 陳　敬上

主題 1

好用句型大補湯

讓教授了解推薦信內容需涵蓋的重點

Law schools value letters from professors that can contribute to their evaluation of whether I would be an asset to the school and whether I would have the academic fortitude to withstand the demanding curriculum. Basically, members of the admission committee are looking to get a well-rounded picture of each candidate with specific examples and details.

法學院在審查申請資料時，很重視教授的推薦函，他們會從推薦函中了解我個人對於該學院是否是個人才，以及了解我有沒有求學的韌性，以應付未來繁重的學業。基本上來說，審查委員偏愛申請者提供全方面完整的資料，包含舉例和細節。

讓教授了解你為何想申請該學院或領域

1. I have always been interested in this field, and have been doing relevant work and thus have had related work experience. I would like to pursue further education so as to acquire expertise in the field.

   我一直對這個領域很感興趣，現在從事的也是相關的工作，累積了相關的工作經驗。我想要進一步求學深造，打造自己在該領域的專業。

2. The university ranks top 10 among law schools in community colleges in America, and it has distinguished professors and wide-range curriculum.

這所大學有美國社區大學第十名的法學院，有傑出的教授群和多元的課程。

3. The school is looking for candidates with leadership, community involvement, analytical, and communication skills. I think I possess such qualities and will be an asset to the school.

這所學校要找的學生須具備領導力，願意參與社區服務，有分析和溝通能力。我認為我具備以上素質，能為該學院帶來很多貢獻。

MEMO

Unit 03 詢問課程

寫作策略

Step 1 **Who** are you writing to? 寫給誰？

Ms. Emma Core

Step 2 **What** courses/programs are you interested in?
對什麼課程有興趣？

Masters of Science in Computer Science

Step 3 **FAQs** (Frequently asked Questions) 常見問題

Admissions, Programs/Units/Courses

Outline 這樣擬

寫信目的　開場先說明有興趣的科系。
細　　節　索取課程細節。
敬請回覆　要求對方收到訊息後回覆確認。
信　　尾　客套語＋署名。

看看老師怎麼寫 🌐

Dear Ms. Emma Core,

I'm very interested in the Master of Environmental Science provided by Faculty of Science, University of Sydney. I'm currently completing my undergraduate degree in Engineering in University of Melbourne, and I'd like to apply to the above postgraduate coursework program upon my graduation. But there are some questions I have regarding the admissions and curriculum.

Regarding admissions, what would be the minimum GPA required to apply to the MES? Do I have to be a Environmental Science undergraduate major to apply? As for the courses, what is the minimum number of units I can take per quarter? What courses can I count as Electives on my program sheet? Last but not least, what classes are offered remotely?

Thank you again for your time with my request, and I would much appreciate if you could reply to the above questions a.s.a.p.

Sincerely,
Oscar Wang

主題 1

中文翻譯

Emma Core女士您好：

我對於雪梨大學的理科碩士學位——環境科學碩士課程很感興趣。我目前還在墨爾本大學就讀工程學學士學位，我想在畢業時申請上述碩士課程，但對於入學條件和課程我有以下這些疑問。

首先跟入學條件有關，要申請環境科學碩士課程的在校平均成績最低要達幾分？是否必須大學主修環境科學系才能申請該碩士課程？至於課程本身，我每一學期最少要修多少學分？在我課程選單上哪些課程算是選修學分？最後，有哪些課程可以透過遠距教學授課？

若您能盡速回答以上疑惑，將不勝感激。

Oscar 王　敬上

關鍵單字片語

1. **faculty**　*n.*　（大學）系、科、學院
   I've just consulted a faculty member regarding the bridging course.
   我剛和系職員諮詢了銜接課程的事宜。

2. **undergraduate**　*adj.*　*n.*　學士；大學部
   She had an undergraduate degree in psychology.
   她有心理學學士學位。

3. postgraduate *adj. n.* 【英】碩士，研究所；【美】博士後

She is currently studying a postgraduate degree in Musical Therapy in University of Melbourne.

她目前正在墨爾本大學攻讀音樂治療的碩士學位。

4. coursework *n.* 授課課程

Most students in Taiwan go to Australia for postgraduate coursework programs.

大部分台灣學生去澳洲攻讀授課型的碩士課程。

5. curriculum *n.* 課程

IT is now on the curriculum in most schools.

資訊科技現在已經是大多數學校的課程之一。

6. elective *n.* 選修學分

Elective units are courses that students can choose to take, but they do not have to take it in order to graduate.

選修學分指的是學生可以選修的學分，但並非取得學位必修的學分。

給力句型解說

現在進行式am/is/are + V-ing

1. 現在說話這一刻正在發生的事。關鍵字now, at the moment。

He **is talking** on the phone **at the moment**. Do you want to wait on the line?

他現在人還在講電話。你想要在線上等候嗎？

2. 雖然非現在這一刻正在動作，但是是這段期間來持續中的事件。關鍵字 currently, this year。

He **is currently taking** a guitar lesson at the music school.

他最近在音樂學校學彈吉他。

3. 來去動詞(go/come/leave/arrive/stay...)以現在進行式代替未來式。

We're going to a movie tonight. Are you coming with us?

我們今晚要去看電影，你要不要一起來？

Last but not least,... 最後一點，…

列舉例子或論點的轉承詞：放在句子前，以逗點隔開。

1. 舉出第一個論點「首先」：to begin with, to start with, first, firstly

2. 舉出第2個或接續的論點「第二、其次、接著、此外」：second, secondly, then, besides, in addition, also, moreover, furthermore, what's more

3. 舉出最後一個論點「最後」：Finally, Last (but not least)

換個對象寫寫看

Dear **Ms. Kelly Lively**,

I'm very interested in **the short-term college study abroad tour in London provided by EF International**. I've read your brochure and online introduction to the program, but there are some questions I have regarding the program details and schedule.

I was wondering if we could join the activities with local students during the tour. I'm also curious about how much time will be on academic classroom learning and how much will be spent touring? What is an optional excursion? How much free time does my group have to organize private tour?

Thank you again for your time with my request and I would much appreciate if you could reply to the above questions a.s.a.p.

Sincerely,
Bruce Wayne

Kelly Lively女士您好：

我對於**EF**國際教育機構舉辦的倫敦短期大學遊學團很感興趣。我已經看過你們的手冊和網路的介紹，但還是有關於課程相關的問題想要詢問您。

我想知道在遊學期間，我們是否可以跟當地學生一起參與活動？我也很想知道會花多少時間在教室上課，以及多少時間旅遊？自選行程又是什麼？我的團有多少時間可以安排私人行程？

若您能盡速回答以上疑惑，將不勝感激。

Bruce Wayne　敬上

主題 1

好用句型大補湯

財務支持

How much does this cost? Whether they're offering financial support to international students? Where can I get information about applying for scholarships? Besides, can the faculty member or the Student Affairs Officer assist me in finding a TA (teaching assistant) or RA(research assistant) position?

我的費用預估要多少，是否提供國際學生財務協助？哪裡可以取得申請獎學金相關的訊息？此外，教員或是學生事務處人員可否協助我找到助教或研究助理的職務？

其他問句

1. I'd like to know what facilities or resources are available to distance learning students.
   我想知道有哪些軟硬體設備或資源提供遠距教學的學生使用。

2. I'm interested in distance learning education in your university. Do you offer distance learning in Fashion Design courses? And what are the requirements for applying online courses?
   我對於貴校的遠距教學課程很感興趣。時裝設計相關的課程是否有開放遠距教學？要申請網路遠距教學的條件是什麼？

3. Will I be able to transfer courses I've already taken at other institutions?
   我是否可以拿我在其他教育機構上過的學分抵扣我該修的學分？

Unit 04 住宿&寄宿家庭

寫作策略

Step 1 **Who** are you writing to? 寫給誰？

Mr. Dennis Wills

Step 2 **What** do you request? 要求什麼？

arranging homestay

Step 3 **Types** of accommodation offered 住宿種類

host families

Step 4 **Questions** 問題

Fees, regulations/rules, location/transportation, host family information, special request

Outline 這樣擬

寫信目的	開場先說明自己入住的時間。
細 節	詢問住宿家庭的細節。
敬請回覆	要求對方收到訊息後回覆確認。
信 尾	客套語+署名。

看看老師怎麼寫

Dear Mr. Wills,

I am writing to inquire about the "English and Homestay Program" provided by HES Language School. I am a college student from Taiwan. I will be coming to New Zealand for three months from June 16th to September 15th 2017. I would like to stay with a host family during my stay, but I have some questions about accommodation arrangement and would like to consult you in advance.

My questions are mainly concerning fees. Do I need to pay homestay placement fee to your institution? Or do you book accommodation for students who sign up for English courses for free? Besides, do I need to pay for airport pick-up? How much do I pay the homestay family every month? Will you help me sign the lease? Do I need to pay security deposit along with my first month's rent at the same time when I arrive? If yes, how much is the deposit? Will I get the full deposit back when I leave?

I would very much appreciate if you can respond to the above questions at your early convenience.

Yours sincerely,
Jessica Ma

 中文翻譯

Wills先生您好：

我寫信詢問有關HES語言學校所提供的「語言課程+寄宿家庭方案」。我是台灣來的大學生。我從2017年6月16日起會到紐西蘭待三個月，從6月16日待到9月15日。我想住在寄宿家庭，但我關於住宿的安排有一些疑問，想要事先跟您諮詢。

我主要的疑問都和費用有關。我要付住宿安排費給你們機構嗎？還是你們對於有報名你們語言課程的學生提供免費住宿安排的服務？此外，我若要求機場接送會需要額外付費嗎？我每個月要付給住宿家庭多少費用？你們會協助我和住宿家庭簽約嗎？我是否要在抵達時先繳第一個月的房租和押金？如果是的話，押金多少錢？等我要離開前，押金會全額退給我嗎？

若您能盡速撥冗回覆以上問題，我將萬分感激。

Jessica 馬 敬上

關鍵單字片語

1. **concerning** *prep.* 關於… (= regarding, about)
   I have several questions regarding the terms of the lease.
   我對於這個房屋租賃契約的條款有一些疑問。

2. **placement** *n.* 安置，安排 (= arrangement)
   The Student Affairs Office charges $20 for dormitory placement for freshmen.

學生事務處針對大一新生安排宿舍會收取美金20元的安置費用。

3. **institution**　*n.*　機構

He just enrolled in an English course at this language institution.

他剛在這家語言學習機構報名了一門英語課程。

4. **sign up for**　註冊；報名 (= enroll in, register)

He's going to sign up for a swimming class.

他將要報名一堂游泳課。

5. **lease**　*n.*　房屋租賃契約

Tenants need to make sure they understand and agree to all the terms in the lease.

房客必須確認了解並同意所有房屋租賃契約上的條款。

6. **security deposit**　押金

How will the landlord return the full amount of security deposit?

房東在什麼條件下會全額退還押金？

給力句型解說

along with + n. 連同

1. **A along with/together with/as well as B**：「A連同B」，主詞是A，決定動詞單複數。

   The security guard **along with** two customers **was** held hostage.

   警衛連同兩位顧客一起被挾持作人質。

   （語法上真正的主詞是the security guard，單數名詞，接單數動詞was。）

2. **(both) A and B**：「A和B」，主詞是A+B，接複數動詞。

The security guard **and** two customers **were** held hostage.

警衛和兩位顧客一起被挾持作人質。

（主詞是the security guard and the two customers，複數名詞，接複數動詞were。）

when + 現在簡單式：代表未來式

從屬連接詞(when, if, after, before, as long as...)引導的子句要用現在簡單式代替未來式。

1. Will I get my full deposit **when I leave**?

   當我離開的時候我能拿回全額押金嗎？

   → 主要子句Will I get my full deposit 保留未來式。

   → 由when引導的附屬子句when I leave 用現在簡單式代替未來式。

2. **If it rains tomorrow**, let's cancel the outdoor barbecue.

   如果明天下雨，我們就取消戶外烤肉。

   → 主要子句let's cancel the outdoor barbecue 保留祈使句。

   → 由If引導的附屬子句If it rains tomorrow 用現在簡單式代替未來式。

換個對象寫寫看 👥

Dear Mr. Josh Whitman,

Thank you for processing my homestay request form promptly. I have received your email yesterday regarding the homestay arrangement. I have read the background information about my host family, Mr. and Mrs. Benjamin Brownings. **But I'd like to know more about them and homestay location.**

Regarding my host family, do they accommodate other international students the same time during my stay? In addition, I have mentioned in my request form that I'm allergic to seafood, and I don't eat beef. Are they OK with my dietary requirements?

I'm also concerned about the location of the homestay. Is it near any public transportation? How long does it take to go to school from the homestay? Is it convenient to get around the city?

I would very much appreciate if you can respond to the above questions at your early convenience.

Yours sincerely,
Jack Peterson

Josh Whitman先生您好：

謝謝您盡速處理了我的寄宿家庭需求表。我昨天收到了您的email，得知您已經為我安排好住宿家庭。我已經讀過我的寄宿家庭主人，Benjamin Brownings夫婦的背景資料。但我想詢問更多有關他們和住宿地點的細節。

關於我的住宿家庭，在我投宿期間，他們是否也接待其他的國際學生呢？此外，我在住宿需求表上有註明我對海鮮過敏且不吃牛肉。他們可以接受我在飲食上面的需求嗎？

我同時也關心我住宿的地點。它是否鄰近公共交通運輸系統？從住宿家庭到

學校大約要花多久時間？要到市區走動是否方便？

若您能盡速撥冗回覆以上問題，我將萬分感激。

Jack Peterson 敬上

好用句型大補湯

關於住宿人員分配、設備和服務相關問題

I have some questions regarding student shared apartments. Do males and females have separate or mixed accommodations? How many people share an apartment? Are there facilities for washing and drying clothes? What appliances are permitted in student rooms? What kinds of housekeeping services are provided?

我對於學生分租公寓有以下的疑問。男生和女生是分開住或混合住宿？多少人一起分租一個公寓？公寓裡有洗衣和乾衣的設備嗎？學生房間內可以攜帶哪些類型的家電用品？是否有提供打掃的服務？

其他問句

1. Is there a meal plan that comes with my housing options?
   住宿方案有沒有結合膳食餐飲相關的配套？

2. Where can I stay if I arrive before or depart after the housing contract begins or ends?
   若我在住宿合約入宿日期前抵達，或合約結束後要多留幾天，我可以住在哪裡？

3. What are the facilities provided in the student residences/apartment/dormitory?
   學生宿舍/公寓內有哪些設備？

4. I'm looking for off campus housing. Where can I find detailed housing listings and landlord reviews? Does the rent include utilities, cable, and internet?
   我在找校外租屋，哪裡可以看到詳細的房屋出租資訊以及房東評價？房租包含水電費、第四台還有網路費嗎？

主題 1

Unit
05
履歷這麼寫

寫作策略

Step **1** **Who** are you writing to? 寫給誰？

Ms. Betty Wang

Step **2** **What** position you are applying for? 申請什麼職位？

administrative assistant

Step **3** **Strength** 強項

educational/academic background, work experience,
skills, awards, extra-curricular activities

Outline 這樣擬

（寫信目的） 開場直接說明你要申請的職務以及自己最相關的專長。

（學經歷背景介紹細節） 分段簡述相關學歷和工作經歷、或熱情展現對於新
工作和該公司的抱負。

（感謝與懇請回覆） 要求對方回覆確認約面試時間。

（信　尾） 客套語＋署名。

看看老師怎麼寫 🌐

Dear Ms. Wang,

I am writing with enthusiasm to apply for the position of administrative assistant listed on 104 Job Bank. I hope you can see from the enclosed resume and CV that I'm perfect and well-qualified for this job.

I majored in English in Fu Jen Catholic University. I have also attached my language proficiency certificates to show that I have good command of English. I also have 3 years of related administrative experience in my previous job, and I'm computer-literate and skilled at routine office work.

I would be very grateful for your consideration, and I am available to come for an interview at your convenience to fully explain my strength and qualifications. You can reach me at 22145212.

I'm looking forward to hearing from you soon.

Sincerely yours,
Emma Liao

主題 1

王小姐您好：

我很熱忱寫信要應徵貴公司在104人力銀行上行政助理一職。我希望您能從我附件的履歷表和個人學經歷列表中看到我能完全勝任，是這份工作的最佳人選。

我在輔仁大學主修英語。我也有附上語言認證資料展現我有絕佳英文能力。我在前一份工作也累積了三年行政相關經驗。我對於電腦使用很上手，也熟悉日常辦公事務。

若能得到您的考慮，我將不勝感激，我也能配合您方便的時間前去面試，以充分解說我的長處和相關經歷。您可以打電話和我聯繫22145212。
期待您的回音。

Emma 廖　敬上

關鍵單字片語

1. **enthusiasm** *n.* 熱忱

   This new employee works with enthusiasm.

   這位新進員工以無比的熱忱工作。

2. **administrative assistant** *n.* 行政助理

   Many college graduates apply for the position of the administrative assistant.

   很多大學畢業生應徵這個行政助理的職缺。

3. **resume** *n.* 履歷

   Cassie tailor-made her resume for the position of project manager.

   Cassie為應徵專案經理的工作，量身訂做寫履歷。

4. **CV (Curriculum Vitae)** *n.* 履歷

   You can send your CV with a cover letter or email asking if they have any vacancies in your trade.

   你可以用介紹信或電子郵件附上你的履歷，詢問他們是否有相關的工作職缺。

5. **certificate** *n.* 證照

   Please enclose a degree certificate to your application form.

   請在你申請書上附上學位證書。

6. **computer-literate** *adj.* 熟悉電腦操作的

   Nowadays almost everyone should be computer-literate to deal with office work.

   現在幾乎人人都要熟悉電腦操作，才能處理辦公室事務。

主題 1

給力句型解說 👉

major in　主修

Sandy majors in Electrical Engineering in college.
Sandy在大學主修電子工程。

in + 領域

1. **minor in　副修**

   She majors in Nursing and minors in Health Management.
   她主修醫護，副修健康管理。

2. **specialize in　專長於**

   This doctor specializes in rehabilitation.
   這位醫生專精復建。

3. **be experienced in　在…方面很有經驗**

   This senior employee is experienced in editing news clips.
   這位資深員工在新聞編輯方面很有經驗。

have a good command of + 語言　　擅長…語言

She was born and raised in Spain, so she has a good command of Spanish.
她在西班牙出生長大，所以她很懂西班牙文。

其他相關句型：

1. **be good at 對…很擅長**

   Mandy is good at translation and interpretation.
   Mandy擅長翻譯與口譯。

主題 1

2. **be skilled at** 對…很擅長

Aboriginal women are skilled in weaving and art craft.

原住民婦女擅長編織與製作手工藝品。

換個對象寫寫看

Dear **Ms. Wang**,

I am interested in the **marketing assistant** position advertised in Times. **I am currently employed as a marketing personnel in XXX company. I have obtained 4 years of marketing experience which are applicable to your requirements for a marketing assistant. My experience in my current job has offered me the opportunity to become familiar with event organizing and brand marketing. I also have extensive experience in public relations. I believe my experiences qualify me for consideration.** To further acquaint you with the specifics of my background, I am enclosing my resume. I hope you will consider me for this position. I look forward to meeting with you and discussing my qualifications in more details.

Sincerely,
Alice Hsu

王小姐您好：
我對於您們在每日時報上刊登應徵行銷助理的工作很感興趣。我目前就在…

公司任職行銷人員。我累積了四年的行銷資歷，符合貴職務的條件要求。

我現職工作提供我機會更熟悉活動的舉辦和品牌行銷。我也對於公關宣傳有很多經驗。我相信這些經驗能讓我成為這份職務的考慮人選。

為讓您更熟悉我相關的背景，我附上我的履歷。希望您能考慮我的應徵。期待能和您見面討論更多我的背景細節。

Alice 徐　敬上

好用句型大補湯

社會新鮮人：強調學業上傑出表現或社團經驗

During my studies at the college, insurance and financial planning are my fields of special interest and expertise. I completed related courses with high grades. And I have obtained various financial certificates, such as Proficiency Test for Financial Planning Personnel. I also participated actively in extra-curricular activities at the university and have gained experiences at organizing events or teamwork and leadership.

在我讀大學期間，保險和財務規劃是我的興趣與專長領域。我以高分修得相關學分。我取得多種財務金融相關證照，例如理財規劃人員專業證照。我也熱衷投入課外社團活動，累積了企劃活動、團體合作以及領導能力。

其他自我推銷的萬用語：

1. 強調經驗與專業：

I have been working in the related field for _____ years and specialize in _____. With thorough knowledge and rich experience, I believe I'm the right man for this position.

我已經在此相關領域工作…年了，專精於…。擁有詳盡的知識和經驗，我相信我是這份職務的最佳人選。

2. 強調對此工作／公司的嚮往與熱忱：

I have long been interested in working for a prestigious company as yours. And your company is at the top of my list of employment consideration.

我對於到像貴公司這樣的一流企業工作很嚮往。貴公司是我求職考慮的首選。

3. 懇請對方參考附件的履歷並給予面試機會：

Please refer to my enclosed resume for more details. I hope you can consider my application.

請詳閱附件的履歷以得到更多資訊。希望您能考慮我的申請。

主題 1

Unit
06
更改面試時間

寫作策略 A B

Step **1** **Who** are you writing to? 寫給誰？

Mr. Dennis Ho

Step **2** **What** position you are applying for? 申請什麼職位？

teaching assistant

Step **3** **Why** do you need to change the date of interview?

為什麼需要改面試時間？

have an exam

Outline 這樣擬

寫信目的	開場先說明感謝對方給予面試機會，但要改時間。
細　節	改時間的原因和自己可以配合的時間。
敬請回覆	要求對方收到訊息後回覆。
信　尾	客套語＋署名

主題 1

看看老師怎麼寫 🌐

Dear Mr. Ho,

Thank you very much for offering me an interview for the position of teaching assistant. I am extremely grateful for this opportunity, but I wonder if it would be possible to change the interview date, as my GEPT-Intermediate level exam is already scheduled for Saturday June 23rd.

I'm available in the afternoons from Monday to Friday. I would be very pleased if you could change the date and give me a chance to be interviewed.

Sincerely yours,
Karen Hsieh

中文翻譯 📝

您好：

謝謝您願意讓我面試助教的職務。我很感激能有這個機會，但我想問是否可以改約其他面試日期，因為我的全民英檢中級考試恰巧也排在6月23日（週六）那一天。

我有空的時間是週一到週五下午的時段。若您能改約面試日期，讓我能去與您面談，我將非常感激。

Karen謝　敬上

關鍵單字片語

1. **grateful** *adj.* 感激的

   I'm very grateful to be offered this position.

   我很感激能得到這個職務。

   gratitude *n.*

2. **opportunity** *n.* 機會 (= chance)

   This is an ideal opportunity to save money on a holiday to Hong Kong.

   這是一個存錢到香港度假的絕佳機會。

3. **wonder** *v.* 想知道

   I was wondering if my application has been processed.

   我想知道我的申請案是否已經被處理了。

4. **date** *n.* 日期

   I'm writing to request for changing the interview date.

   我寫信來請求更改面試時間。

5. **schedule** *v.* 排定行程

   The flight is scheduled to depart at 5:00 sharp.

   這班飛機預定五點整起飛。

6. **available** *adj.* 有空的

   Are you available for an interview this Friday afternoon at 2:00 pm?

   你本週五下午兩點是否有空可以來面試？

給力句型解說

it is possible for 人 to V　　人做…是可能的

It's possible for people to migrate to another planet.
人類去外太空殖民是可能的。

延伸句型：**it is + adj. + for人 to V**　　做…是…的
It's convenient for people all over the world to meet online with the help of Internet.
拜網路所賜，世界各地的人要在網路上見面很方便。

if + 間接問句　　是否

間接問句：一個問句併入另一個句子中者，稱為間接問句。

句型：主要子句 + 疑問詞 (無疑問詞就用if/whether) + S +V

1. Who is he?（直接問句）
   I don't know **who he is**.（間接問句）
2. What do you want?（直接問句）
   Tell me **what you want**.（間接問句）── do不見了
3. What does he want?（直接問句）
   Do you know **what he wants**?（間接問句）── does/did併入動詞
4. Does he like you?（直接問句）
   I'm wondering **if he likes you**.（間接問句）── 沒疑問詞就用if/whether當疑問詞

換個對象寫寫看

Dear **Ms. Liao**,

I'm very grateful to be granted an interview for the position of **editor of sports news**. I've been reading your newspaper for years and have always dreamed of working as an editor in your company. **However, I'm still working a full-time job and find it hard to take a day off for the scheduled interview.** I was wondering if it would be possible to change the interview date to next Monday afternoon.

I would be very pleased if you could change the date and give me a chance to talk with you regarding the position.

Sincerely yours,
Betty Chang

廖小姐您好：

謝謝您願意讓我面試體育新聞編輯的職務。我很感激能有這個機會。我多年來一直是貴報紙忠實讀者，也一直夢想有一天能在你們公司工作。但由於我現在還有份全職的工作，原本預定要面試的那一天很難請假。我想問是否可以改約面試日期到下週一下午。

若您能改約面試日期，讓我能過去與您面談，我將非常感激。

Betty張　敬上

好用句型大補湯

仍在工作中，無法請假面試

Currently, I'm still working, and thus I'm only available for the interview on Thursday afternoons. I would be very grateful if I can meet you then for the interview.

我現在仍在工作，因此我唯一有空的時間就是星期四下午。若能選擇該時段與您見面，我將非常感激。

當天有私人事務要處理

Due to some urgent private matters that I need to deal with, I can only request to change the assigned interview date. I'm very interested in this position and sincerely hope I can still have a chance to be interviewed.

因為突發的私人事務要處理，我只能跟您請求更改面試日期。我對這個職務很有興趣，希望還是有機會可以跟您面試。

其他常見句型：

1. I am extremely grateful for offering me an interview, but I wonder if it would be possible to change the interview date, as ... .
   我很感激您給我面試的機會，但我想知道有無可能更改面試日期，因為……。

2. I am very sorry that I'm not able to attend the interview on the scheduled date since I can't take a day off work.
   我很抱歉沒辦法依原定的時間來面試，因為當天我無法請假。

主題 1

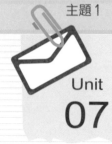

Unit 07 詢問面試結果

寫作策略 🄰🄱

Step **1** **Who** are you writing to? 寫給誰？

Mr. Nate Truman

Step **2** **What** position did you apply for? 申請什麼職務？

marketing personnel

Step **3** **When** did you have an interview with the interviewer?
哪時的面試？

Last Monday on June 25th

Step **4** **What** did you discuss in the interview?
面試時討論了什麼？

Background and work experiences, duties of the
position, salary requirements

Outline 這樣擬 ✏️

寫信目的　開場先說明感謝對方撥冗與你面談，說明面試的職務與日期以提醒對方。

詢　　問	客氣提醒對方能回應是否已決定要錄取自己。
敬請回覆	請求對方收到訊息後儘快回覆確認。
信　　尾	客套語＋署名。

看看老師怎麼寫

Dear Mr. Truman,

Thank you so much for taking time out of your tight schedule to interview me last Monday for the position of the marketing **personnel**. It was my pleasure to sit down and discuss my future possibilities with such a **well-established** corporation as **yours**. I was very impressed with the **potential** of your company and sincerely hope I can **contribute to marketing** the new **lines** of products.

However, I haven't heard from you since the interview. I'm wondering if the final decision has been made regarding this position. I believe my experiences in marketing can be a great addition to this job and hope my application can be reconsidered.

Thank you again and look forward to hearing from you soon.

Sincerely,
Andrew Whitman

中文翻譯

Truman先生您好：

謝謝您上週一百忙之中抽空和我面試有關行銷人員的職務。貴公司信譽卓越，能坐下來與您討論我的未來發展，是我的榮幸。我也對貴公司的發展潛力留下深刻的印象，希望我能貢獻一己之力，有機會協助行銷最新系列的產品。

但從面試結束後到現在我還沒收到您的回覆。我想知道這份職務是否已經有定案了？我相信以我在行銷的經驗，必定能在該職務上帶來很大的助益，希望您能再考慮一下我的應徵。

再次感謝您，希望能盡快得到您的消息。

Andrew Whitman　敬上

關鍵單字片語

1. **personnel**　*n.*　員工 (=staff, employee)
   All personnel are to receive security badges.
   所有職員都要佩帶識別證。

2. **well-established**　*adj.*　發展健全的；信譽卓越的
   She works in a well-established non-profit organization.
   她在一個發展健全的非營利組織工作。

3. **potential**　*n.*　潛力
   A lot of ordinary people display their potentials in the talent

show.

很多素人在達人秀中展現他們的潛能。

4. contribute　*v.*　對…有所貢獻 (+to)

I believe I can contribute a lot to this position and hope my application can be considered.

我相信自己可以在這個職務一展長才，希望我的應徵可以被考慮。

5. market　*v.*　行銷

She has gained lots of practical experience in marketing and public relations.

她在行銷和公關上累積很多實務經驗。

6. line　*n.*　系列

The designer brand has just launched its new lines of jeans.

這個設計師品牌剛推出新的一系列牛仔褲。

給力句型解說

contribute to　對…作出貢獻；捐款

1. 主詞 + contribute to + 名詞/V-ing

This professor has **contributed** a lot **to the research** of cure for AIDS.

這位教授對於愛滋病解藥的研究貢獻良多。

He has **contributed** a lot **to raising** these adopted children.

他為扶養這些認養的孩子貢獻了很多。

2. 主詞 + contribute + 受詞 + to + 名詞/V-ing

The millionaire **contributed half of his savings to charities**.

這位百萬富翁將他一半的積蓄捐給慈善團體。

所有格代名詞

	所有格形容詞 + 名詞	= 所有格代名詞
我的	my + n.	= mine
你（們）的	your + n.	= yours
他的	his + n.	= his
她的	her + n.	= hers
它的	its + n.	= its
我們的	our + n.	= ours
他們的	their + n.	= theirs

常見「所有格代名詞」使用時機：代換句子前半段提到的名詞。

1. 比較級的前後名詞：

   My car is better than **yours**. (= **your car**)

   我的車比你的（車）來的好。

2. **a +** 名詞 **+ of +**所有格代名詞：

   He is a friend of **mine** (= **my friends**).

   他是我的一個朋友。

換個對象寫寫看

主題 1

Dear **Ms. Erwin**,

Thank you so much for offering me an interview **two weeks ago** for the position of **the executive assistant**. I'm eager to work in your company, and I sincerely believe I can be a great asset for this position.

However, I haven't received any reply from you regarding the outcome of your decision so far. I'm writing this letter to display my strong ambition and desire for this position and hope to hear from you as soon as possible.

Thank you again for your time and your reconsideration will be highly appreciated.

Sincerely,
Bill Jackson

Erwin女士您好：
感謝您兩週前給我機會面試行政助理一職。我很希望能在貴公司工作，相信自己可以成為此職務的主力。
但到現在我還沒收到您的面試結果的決定。我寫信來展現我對這個職務的抱負與想望，希望能盡速得到您的回覆。
再次謝謝您寶貴的時間，若您能再考慮一下我的應徵，將十分感激。

Bill Jackson 敬上

好用句型大補湯

提醒對方曾經答應過你在某個日期前給你回音

During the interview, you mentioned that I would be informed of the result of my application before June 30th. It's already July 7th, but I haven't heard any information from you. I'm sending this letter to show my ambition and interest in this position and hopefully you can reconsider my application.

在面試時，您有提到會在6月30日前通知我應徵的結果。但今天已經是7月7日，我還沒收到您的回覆。我寫信來展現我對這份職務的抱負與興趣，希望您能重新考慮我的應徵。

重申自己適合這份職務，展現企圖心，期盼對方可以主動和自己聯絡

I am very eager to work in your company. I strongly believe I am the best man for this position since I have thorough knowledge of the field and have accumulated practical hands-on experiences. Please don't hesitate to contact me for further information. I hope I can be reconsidered for this job.

我很期待能在貴公司工作。我也相信以我對這領域的通盤知識和過去累積的實務經驗，讓我成為這份工作的最佳人選。請不吝和我聯繫，讓我能提供您更多的資料。希望我的應徵能再次被考慮。

其他詢問面談結果的萬用句：

1. I'm sending this letter to ask if you have further questions regarding my application, and your timely consideration would be highly appreciated.

   我寫信來詢問您是否對於我的應徵有其他的問題，您若能考慮我的應徵，本人將感激不盡。

2. I'm writing to inquire the outcome of my interview last Friday. I'm very anxious to know your answer, and your prompt reply would be highly appreciated.

   我寫信來詢問有關上週五面試的結果。我很急著想要知道您的答案。若您您盡快回覆，我將十分感激。

3. Thank you for your time and consideration for my application. Please feel free to contact me once the final decisions are made regarding this position.

   謝謝您寶貴的時間與考慮我的應徵。若您做好決定，歡迎與我連絡。

主題2
業務跑跑跑，採購Go廠商！

Unit
01

約定拜訪時間

寫作策略 Ⓐ Ⓑ

Step **1** **Who** are you writing to? 寫給誰？

Mr. Josh Thomas

Step **2** **What** is this email for? 主旨

business appointment letter: to make an appointment

Step **3** **When** did you last contact? 最後何時接觸？

this Monday's Trade Fair

Step **4** **Why** do you want to make a business appointment?
面談原因

make a presentation

Step **5** **Schedule** a meeting date/time 約面談時間

to suit the customer's availability/convenience

Outline 這樣擬

寒暄簡介　開場提醒上次曾見面或談話，點出自己公司和對方興趣的主力商品。

邀約面談　熱情提出希望見面進一步介紹商品或提供服務。

感謝與懇請回覆　要求對方回覆確認約面試時間。

信　　尾　客套語＋署名。

看看老師怎麼寫

主題 2

Dear Mr. Thomas,

I would like you to know how much I enjoyed talking to you on Monday's trade fair. And I'm very delighted to know our company's latest surveillance software, No Leak, has made a great impression. Transparent Technologies Inc. has been in business for more than 30 years developing high-tech software for office usages. No Leak is indeed the best security software ever developed to protect valuable customer information and transaction data.

To make you acquainted with this software, I was wondering if we could have a business meeting, so I can pay you a visit to further demonstrate to you and your associates how this software works.

It would be our pleasure to meet you at your convenience. Please kindly suggest the appointment time. Feel free to contact me at

4556346260 or drop me email at faltu@zalaltu.com.

I am looking forward to having a chance to meet you again.

Yours truly,
Allen B Bennett

中文翻譯

Thomas先生您好：

我想讓您知道我在星期一的商展上和您相談甚歡。我很開心本公司最新的監視軟體No Leak讓您留下很好的印象。本公司Transparent科技已經在業界30餘年，發展辦公室用高科技軟體。而No Leak是我們開發最棒的資料保全軟體，可以保護重要的客戶資料和交易資訊。

為了讓您更熟悉這一款軟體，我想詢問我們是否可以約個商業訪談，讓我可以拜訪您，進一步向您和您的合夥人展示如何使用這套軟體。

若能在您有空的時間跟您見面，將是我們的榮幸。請建議面訪時間。歡迎與我電話聯繫或回傳電子郵件。

期待有機會和您再見面。

Allen B Bennett　敬上

關鍵單字片語

1. **trade fair** *n.* 商展；貿易展

   These company representatives exchange their business cards at the trade fair.

   這些公司的代表在商展上彼此交換名片。

2. **be in business** 營業

   This furniture retailer has been in business for decades.

   這間家具零售商已經營業幾十年了。

3. **transaction** *n.* 金錢交易

   The bank charges a fixed rate for each transaction.

   銀行會對每一筆交易收取固定的手續費。

4. **be acquainted with** 對…熟悉 (= be familiar with)

   She's well acquainted with the process of visa application.

   她對於簽證申請流程很熟悉。

5. **pay someone a visit** 拜訪某人 (=visit)

   May I pay you a visit tomorrow morning to offer free sampling session of our yogurt?

   我可以明天拜訪您提供優格的免費試吃活動嗎？

6. **associate** *n.* 合夥人

   One of his business associates ran away with millions of dollars.

   他的一位合夥人捲款數百萬逃走了。

主題 2

給力句型解說

A + make/leave/create + a + adj. + impression + on B　A給B留下⋯的印象

This interviewee made a good impression on the employer.
這位面試者給雇主留下不錯的印象。

延伸觀念：

B have a + adj. + impression + of + A　B對A的印象⋯

The employer had a good impression of the interviewee.
雇主對這位面試者的印象不錯。

人 + have the impression that +子句　人印象中認為⋯

Most people have the impression that products made in China must be in poor quality.
大部分的人印象中覺得中國大陸製作的產品品質一定很差。

主詞 is the +最高級 + (that) + 現在完成式　主詞⋯是⋯過最⋯

主詞 is the +最高級 + (that) S + have/has ever + p.p → that子句接主動語態

This is the best movie **(that) I have ever seen**.
這是我看過最棒的電影。

主詞 is the +最高級 + ever + p.p → that子句接被動語態，只保留過去分詞

This is the best software **ever developed**.

= This is the best software **that has ever been developed**.
這是被開發過最棒的軟體。

換個對象寫寫看

Dear **Ms. Lai**,

I enjoyed talking to you **on Monday's meeting** and was very excited to know your company will launch a new line of jewelry in 3 months and is in need for marketing campaigns. I'm very pleased to inform you that our company has been in business for more than 15 years, providing brand marketing strategies. We're very confident that our experiences in event organizing and public relations can assist in enhancing brand awareness and boosting customer loyalty.

To make you acquainted with our services, I was wondering if we could have a business meeting to discuss on the partnership. I was wondering if you could squeeze some time next Tuesday. Please feel free to contact me at 271564652 or email me at greatimpression@yahoo.com.
I am looking forward to meeting you.

Yours truly,
Melody Chen

主題 2

賴小姐您好：

在星期一的會議上和您相談甚歡。我很開心知道貴公司再過3個月要發表最新系列的珠寶品牌，且正在需要宣傳活動。我很榮幸要跟您說本公司已經在業界15年，提供品牌行銷策略。我們有信心我們在活動策劃以及公關活動上的經驗可以協助增加品牌識別度和顧客忠誠度。

為了讓您更熟悉我們的服務，我想詢問是否我們可以約個商業訪談，討論合作計畫，我想知道下週二您是否可以空出時間。歡迎與我電話聯繫或回電子郵件。

期待有機會和您見面。

Melody陳 敬上

好用句型大補湯

已約好會面時間：再次確認或提醒時間，並提供會議資料

This letter is in response to the telephonic conversation we had last Saturday regarding our business meeting. I am writing to confirm our appointment on February 15th at 4:00 pm in your office, in which I will make a presentation to demonstrate our marketing campaign proposal for your latest cosmetics. Please go through the enclosed proposal and suggest if any changes are required.

這封信是回應上週六我們在電話裡討論要約的商務會議。我寫信來確認會議

時間是2月15日下午4點在您的辦公室，會議上我會做簡報，展示我們為推廣貴公司化妝品所設計的行銷企劃案。請先過目附件的企劃案內容，並指出是否有需要修正之處。

其他約面談時間的萬用語：

1. I'm writing to make an appointment with you for next Monday.
   我寫信來和您約下週一面談。

2. I was wondering if it would be convenient to meet you tomorrow.
   我想問若明天和您會面是否方便。

3. Would it be convenient if I pay you a visit this Friday afternoon?
   本週五下午去拜訪您是否方便？

4. Could you arrange an appointment with Mr. Green for me?
   您是否能幫我安排和Green先生會晤？

5. I'd like to drop by tomorrow to talk over our plan.
   我想要明天去您那一趟，討論我們的計畫。

6. I look forward to seeing you at your office on July 18th.
   期待7月18日和您在您辦公室會晤。

7. Could you squeeze in some time for me next week?
   下週您是否可以挪出時間和我見面？

主題 2

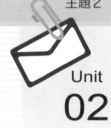

Unit 02 詢問合作機會

寫作策略 A B

Step 1 **Who** are you writing to? 寫給誰？

Mr. Jason Hardi

Step 2 **What** services/products do you offer? 提供的服務

provide cleaning services for hotels or office complex

Step 3 **When** did you last contact? 最後何時接觸？

this Monday's business meeting

Step 4 **Why** do you write this email? 寫信原因

form partnership

Step 5 **What's** the strength of your product/services? 產品特色

high quality at low price, supervisors, list of reference

Outline 這樣擬

寫信致謝 開場先感謝對方給予面談合作的機會。

公司與產品強項　強調給客戶的產品或服務優勢。

敬請回覆　要求對方收到訊息後回覆。

信　　尾　客套語＋署名。

看看老師怎麼寫

Dear Mr. Hardi,

Thank you very much for letting me meet with you and your associates on Monday. I hope you have time to look over our proposal to provide cleaning services for Linslade Office Complex which I brought you on Monday.

As I mentioned when we met, we take extra care to ensure that your office suites receive the finest services possible at reasonable costs. Our team of supervisors constantly evaluate the products and techniques that we use and inspect the work done by our cleaning staff. What's more, they check with your office tenants on a monthly basis to make sure the work is being done to their satisfaction. Please feel free to check anyone on the list I provide you with. I'm certain that all our corporate clients are pleased with our work.

I'd like to stop by with a contract this Friday if possible, so that we can start brightening the office environment the Linslade Office Complex on the first of next month.

主題 2

Looking forward to being at your service soon.

Sincerely yours,
Sandy Chih

中文翻譯

Hardi先生您好：

謝謝您讓我週一有機會可以和您以及您的合夥人面談。希望您已經先過目過我當天帶給您看的合作企劃案，了解我們可以為貴商務大樓提供的清掃服務。

就如我當天會晤時所提到的，我們用心確保辦公大樓各樓房都能以合理的花費獲得最好的清潔服務。我們的監督團隊時常評估我們使用的產品和技術，以及巡視清潔人員的作業。此外，他們也會每月和貴大樓的住戶確認他們滿意我們的清潔品質。我附上一份用戶推薦名單，歡迎您和名單上有使用我們服務的用戶作聯繫。我確信所有和我們合作過的客戶都很滿意我們的品質。

如果可以的話，我想要本週五到貴公司一趟給您一份合約書，這樣我們最快下個月一號就可以開始為貴辦公大樓打掃環境了。

希望能盡快為您服務。

Sandy秦　敬上

關鍵單字片語

1. **look over** 檢視 (= check)

   The supervisor looked over my proposal and gave me some instructions for revision.

   主管檢視過我的企劃案並給我修改的指示。

2. **ensure** *v.* 確保 (= make sure)

   I double checked my resume to ensure there's no grammatical or spelling errors.

   我反覆檢查我的履歷，確保沒有文法或拼字錯誤。

3. **technique** *n.* 技術

   They have state-of-the-art techniques in renovating buildings.

   他們有高超的技術翻修建築物。

4. **on a ...basis** 以…的頻率

   My professor discusses with me regarding my thesis on a regular basis.

   我的指導教授定期和我討論我的論文。

5. **client** *n.* 客戶 (= customer)

   I'm a regular client of this fine dining restaurant.

   我是這家高檔餐廳的常客。

6. **stop by** 順道拜訪

   I'll stop by Uncle Sam and bring him your regards.

   我會順道拜訪山姆叔叔並代你向他問候。

主題 2

給力句型解說 👆

使役動詞

A + let B + 原型動詞　　A讓B做…

The parents won't **let** their daughter **go** on a date alone.
這對父母不讓他們的女兒單獨出外約會。

A + have/make + B + 原型動詞　A要求命令B去做= A ask/tell/get + B + to V

Mom **made** me **sweep** the floor last night.
= Mom **asked me to sweep** the floor last night.
媽媽昨晚叫我掃地。

at + 時間／速度／價錢／代價　　以…的花費

You can get a chic haircut **at a very reasonable cost**.
你可以以合理的價錢剪一頭流行的髮型。

You can enjoy fine dining **at a very affordable price** at this restaurant.
在這間餐廳你可以以負擔的起的價格吃到精緻的餐點。

A high-speed camera can capture any movement **at the speed of** light.
高速攝影機可以以光速的速度捕捉任何的動作。

換個對象寫寫看

Dear **Ms. Anderson**,

Thank you very much for letting me meet with you on **Monday**. I am very excited to learn that you are opening more English teaching institutes all over Taiwan and is in need of fast and reliable services for recruiting qualified teachers.

A lot of ESL schools feel that finding a good teacher is difficult. **This is where we at Reach and Teach come in. Our motto is matching great teachers with great schools. We carefully screen all job applicants to ensure our teachers possess satisfactory teaching qualifications and skills.**

I have faith that we can form a successful business partnership, and please kindly reply to this email and tell me what you think about the proposal we brought you on Monday.

Looking forward to hearing from you soon.

Sincerely yours,
Claire Wen

Anderson女士您好：

謝謝您讓我週一有機會可以和您面談。我很高興得知您計畫要在全台灣開設更多語言教學機構，且需要快速可靠的師資仲介服務。

主題 2

很多語言學校發現要找到好老師是很困難的，而這就是我們**Reach and Teach**公司切入協助的部分。我們的座右銘就是幫好老師找到好的學校。我們細心審查每位求職者的背景，確保我們仲介的老師都有令人滿意的教學背景或技巧。

我相信我們可以建立很成功的合作關係。請回覆此郵件讓我知道您對於週一我們帶去的企劃案的想法。

希望能盡快得到您的回音。

Claire溫 敬上

好用句型大補湯

附上合約，再約見面討論合約的細節

Please find enclosed a copy of the contract for your reference. If possible, I'd like to schedule another meeting with you to discuss the contract and see if we agree with all the terms and conditions. We look forward to building partnership with you and I'm certain you will be pleased with our services.

請看附件供您參考的合約書。如果可能的話，我想要跟您再約個時間見面討論合約，確認我們是否同意裡面所有的條約。我很希望能和您建立合作關係，也相信您一定會滿意我們的服務。

其他詢問有無合作可能的句型：

1. It would be our pleasure to be at your service.
   若能為您服務，將是我們的榮幸。

2. I'm writing this letter to inquire your feedback and comments on the proposal for mutual cooperation.
   我寫信來詢問您對於雙方合作企劃案的回應。

3. Please don't hesitate to contact me regarding any questions in the terms and conditions of the contract.
   若您對於合約細節有任何疑問，請不吝與我聯繫。

4. I have faith that we can form a successful business partnership, and any of your suggestion and comments are welcome as to how we can cooperate.
   我相信我們一定可以共創好的合作關係，歡迎提出任何對於如何合作的建議和想法。

主題 2

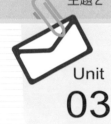

Unit 03 確認訂單內容

寫作策略 AB

S tep 1　**Who** are you writing to? 寫給誰？

Mr. July Woodson

S tep 2　**What** is the email for? 主旨

confirm an order

S tep 3　**features** in your email confirmation 內容

thank the customer for the order, order number, shipping information

Outline 這樣擬

寫信目的	開場先說明感謝對方下訂單。
細　節	訂單品項等細節確認。
敬請回覆	請求對方收到訊息後儘快回覆確認並付款。
信　尾	客套語＋署名。

看看老師怎麼寫

Dear Ms. Woodson,

Thank you for shopping at xyz.com. Depending on your location and shipping method, you should receive your product(s) within 3 to 5 business days after we confirm your payment.

Order Number: 10320
Order Date: Friday October 30, 2015
Payment Method: Secure Credit Card
Products:
2 x Long-sleeved Wool Sweater (L, Purple) $19.98/each
Sub-Total: $39.96
United Parcel Service (shipping fee): $11.42
Total: $51.38
Shipping Address:
No. 123 Pine St. New York, NY 10001 United States
Billing Address:
Same as above

Please confirm this order and make the payment at your earliest convenience.

Sincerely,
Andy Curton

中文翻譯

Woodson小姐您好：

謝謝您在XYZ網站上下訂單。根據您的送貨地址和運輸方式，您會在我們收到費用後3到5個工作天內收到您訂購的商品。

訂單代號：10320

訂貨日期：2015年10月30日

付款方式：安全的信用卡

訂購商品明細：

2件長袖羊毛毛衣（L尺碼，紫色）　單件價格19.98美元

小計：39.96美元

聯邦貨運服務（運費）：11.42美元

總計：51.38美元

送貨地址：松樹街123號，紐約，美國，區域號碼10001

發票地址：同上

請確認以上訂單無誤，並請您盡快付費。

Andy Curton　敬上

關鍵單字片語

1. **location** *n.* 位置

   The hotel is situated in a perfect location overlooking the lake.

   這間旅館位置絕佳，眺望整個湖景。

2. **method** *n.* 方式 (= way, means)

   There are various payment methods to choose from when you shop online.

   在網路上購物，有多種付款方式可供選擇。

3. **business day** 工作天

   The customer service staff will contact me within two business days.

   客服人員會在兩個工作天內和我聯繫。

4. **sub-total** *n.* 小計

   The sub-total amount doesn't include shipping fees or taxes.

   小計的費用不包含運費和稅。

5. **parcel** *n.* 包裹

   The parcel arrived two days after I made the order.

   包裹在我訂貨後兩天送達。

6. **billing address** 帳單寄送地址

   The billing address is the same as the shipping address.

   帳單寄送地址和收貨地址一樣。

主題 2

給力句型解說 👉

depend on　由……決定

Whether the outdoor barbecue will be held depends on the weather.

室外烤肉是否會舉辦由天候決定。

延伸句型：

depend on/ rely on/ count on 依賴

Children depend on their parents for food and shelter.

孩子依賴父母取得食物和庇護。

the same as ...　和……一樣

My cell phone is the same as yours.

我的手機和你的一樣。

延伸句型：

the same +名詞 + as ...

My cell phone has the same features as yours.

我的手機和你的功能一樣。

換個對象寫寫看 👥

Dear **Ms. Chen**,

Thank you for shopping at easybuy.com. We have received your

purchase order for the following.

Order Number: 105200

Order Date: Friday October 30, 2015

2 X microwave oven NT$3500/each

1 X washing machine NT$15000/each

Sub-Total: NT$22000

Shipping Service (ground): NT$700

Total: NT$22700

Payment Method: Credit Card

Shipping Address:

2F No. 25 Ming Chuang East Road, Taipei City

Billing Address:

Same as above

Please confirm this order and make the payment within three days of orders. The products are expected to be delivered within 5 business days after confirmation of payment.

Sincerely,

Jennifer Wu

陳小姐您好：

謝謝您在**easybuy**網站上下訂單。我們已收到以下您的訂單。

訂單代號：105200

訂貨日期：2015年10月30日

訂購商品明細：

2台微波爐　單品價格台幣3500元

主題 2

1台洗衣機　單品價格台幣15000元

小計：台幣22000元

貨運服務（運送到一樓）台幣700元

總計：台幣22700元

付款方式：信用卡

送貨地址：台北市民權東路25號2樓

發票地址：同上

請確認以上訂單無誤，並請您在三日內付費。貨品會在確認收到貨款後**5**個工作天內送達。

Jennifer 吳　敬上

好用句型大補湯

告知客戶已經收到貨款，正在出貨中

We also received the payment of $51.38 in form of ATM transaction on Feb. 28th. The items are being sent to the address as mentioned in the letter of order. The items are expected to be delivered on within the 5 or 6 days of receipt of orders. The statement of orders and bill along with the warranty documents will be delivered along with the items.

我們也已經在2月28日收到您ATM轉帳的51.38美金貨款。您所訂購的商品正出貨到收貨地址。預計在我們收到訂單後5到6個工作天送達。訂單明細、帳單、以及保固文件也會跟著貨品一併送達。

其他訂單確認信件萬用句：

1. We are thankful for the order and pleased to serve you. We hope that your association with us will continue in the future, too.
   我們很感謝您的訂單，也很榮幸能為您服務。希望您未來也能繼續向我們訂貨。

2. Any defects in the items or any problems with the statement of orders must be reported at the earliest.
   任何商品的瑕疵或訂單明細的問題請盡速和我們反應。

3. The invoice is enclosed, along with an order form for next year's catalog. We sincerely hope you can continue utilizing our services.
   附上發票，以及明年型錄的訂單。我們竭誠歡迎您能持續使用我們的服務。

4. Please kindly make the payment within 3 days and keep us informed once the payment is done. Order will be canceled if no payment is received within three days of ordering.
   請在3天內付款，付款後也請通知我們。若下訂單起三天內沒有收到款項，訂單自動取消。

主題 2

Unit 04 詢價與折扣

寫作策略 A B

Step 1 **Who** are you writing to? 對象？
Mr. Josh Thomas

Step 2 **How** did you hear of the company/product? 如何得知？
the ad on newspaper, magazines

Step 3 **What** do you want to obtain? 希望獲得的資訊？
a catalog, quotation, request for an offer, time of shipment, discount

Step 4 **What** will you do if you can accept the quotation/offer? 後續發展
place an order, sign a long-term contract

Outline 這樣擬

寫信目的 開場自我介紹，點出對該公司產品有興趣，想要詢價。

請教細節 請對方具體報價，提供商品價格、數量、規格、單位、裝船貨運時間、付款方式等細節。

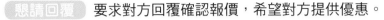

懇請回覆　要求對方回覆確認報價，希望對方提供優惠。
信　　尾　客套語+署名。

 看看老師怎麼寫

Dear Mr. Thomas,

We are the manufacturer of instant coffee powder. Your ad of coffee beans on Money Daily interests us. We'd like to receive the latest catalog of all your coffee beans and powder, as well as the details of the lowest quotation you can offer and the terms of payment.

Please quote us your best offer for coffee beans per kilogram and the discount you can allow. We will also find it more helpful if you can supply samples. In addition, we'd like to inquire if we can purchase online.

I am looking forward to hearing from you soon.

Yours truly,
Juliet Browning

主題 2

 中文翻譯

Thomas先生您好：

我們是即溶咖啡粉製造商。您在金錢日報上的咖啡豆廣告讓我們很感興趣。我們想取得你們最新的咖啡豆和咖啡粉產品型錄，以及您的最低報價和付款說明等細節。

請給我們每公斤咖啡豆的最低報價，以及你們可以提供的優惠。若您能提供樣品，那就更有幫助了。此外，我們也想詢問是否可以在網路上訂購。

期待盡快收到您的回覆。

Juliet Browning 敬上

關鍵單字片語

1. **manufacturer**　*n.*　製造商
   The manufacturer of organic cosmetics dedicates to using organic natural materials.
   這個有機化妝品製造商致力於使用有機的天然材料。
2. **catalog**　*n.*　型錄
   This catalog fully illustrates the medical benefit of the herbal tea.
   這個型錄充分說明這款花草茶的醫療功效。
3. **quotation**　*n.*　報價

May I have the lowest quotation of your products?

我可不可以請您針對產品給我最優惠的報價？

4. **term**　*n.*　條款

Both companies are still negotiating regarding the terms in the contract.

兩個公司對於合約條款還在研討中。

5. **discount**　*n.*　折扣

I can get discount if I buy in large quantities.

如果我大量購買可以享有優惠。

6. **supply**　*v.*　提供 (=offer, provide)

I was wondering if the manufacturer could supply products in large quantities.

我想知道製造商是否可以大量供貨。

給力句型解說

> **A + 單音節形容詞 -er　　+ than B　　比較級**
> **more + 多音節形容詞**

1. **than + 主格 或 受格**

You are taller than I. = You are taller than me.

You are taller than I am.（此處不得用受格）

你比我高。

I like you better than he (likes you).

與主格比較：我喜歡你勝過他喜歡你。

I like you better than (I like) him.

與受格比較：我喜歡你勝過我喜歡他。

主題 2

2. 比較的對象要同性質

Your pencil is longer than mine. (=my pencil.)

你的筆比我（的筆）長。

The weather in Taiwan is hotter than that(=the weather) in Japan.

台灣的天氣比日本（的天氣）熱。

People in Kaohsiung are more generous than those (=people) in Taipei.

高雄人比台北（人）熱情。

A + be + the單音節形容詞est　+ in 地區/of團體　最高級
the most + 多音節形容詞

The elephant is the biggest animal in the zoo.

大象是動物園裡最大的動物。

This one is the most expensive of all the cars in the store.

這部車是店裡最貴的一輛。

 換個對象寫寫看

Dear **Sir or Madam**,

I'm in charge of purchasing air conditioners for all our school classrooms, and I'm interested in buying in large quantity with you directly. **We'd like to get the latest catalog of all models available, with detailed description of features and prices. And please make the best offer and discount you can allow since we will purchase about 32 to 35 air conditioners.**

We'd also like to know if you can provide free shipping and free installation services of the air conditioners. In addition, can we pay in 24-month installments with 0% interest rate?

If the prices, quality of products and services are acceptable, we will consider purchasing in large quantity.

Hope to hear from you soon.

Yours truly,
Peter Cruise

敬啟者：
我負責採買我們學校所有教室的冷氣。對於直接和您大宗採購很有興趣。
我們想要您所有機種的型錄，要有詳細的性能說明和報價。既然我們會大宗採購**32**到**35**台冷氣，請給我最優惠的價格和折扣。

我們也想知道您是否提供免費冷氣運送和安裝服務。此外我們是否可以24期零利率分期付款？

如果價格、品質和服務都可以接受，我們就會考慮大量訂購。

期待盡快收到您的回覆。

Peter Cruise 敬上

好用句型大補湯 📋

需從海外進口的物品

Please send us the quotation per kilogram C&F Taipei, Taiwan, including insurance, handling, and freight. We'd also like to know the minimum export quantities and the time of shipment.

請給我們貨物運到台灣台北的到貨價，包含保險、手續費和運費。我們也想要詢問出口最低進貨量，以及貨運時間。

提醒最晚報價期限

Since we have already made an inquiry of all your articles, would you please make an offer by the end of this week? We'd like to know the prices (exclusive of tax) of all your products.

既然我們已經向您的產品詢價過，可否能請您在本週末前給我們不含稅的報價？我們想要知道您所有產品的不含稅報價。

其他詢價的萬用句型：

1. Please quote us the lowest price for all the items listed hereunder.

   請針對以下品項給我們最低的報價。

2. I'd like to have your lowest offer/quotations for the ink cartridge.

   我想要知道您們墨水匣的最低報價。

3. Prices quoted should include freight to Taiwan and insurance.
   報價請包含到台灣的運費以及保險。

4. Please keep us informed of the latest quotation of the following articles.
   請告知我們以下品項的最新報價。

5. We would highly appreciate if you can forward the latest samples along with best prices.
   若您能附上最新的樣品以及最優惠的報價，我們將非常感激。

6. Please also inform me how this offer remains firm/open.
   也請告知這個報價有效期間有多長。

7. Full/Detailed information regarding prices, quality, quantity available, and other particulars would be very appreciated.
   若能詳列價格、品質、供貨數量以及其他條件，將會讓我十分感激。

主題 2

Unit
05
以量制價

寫作策略

Step 1　**Who** are you writing to? 對象？

Ms. Eileen Cooper

Step 2　**What** is this email for? 主旨

counter offer

Step 3　**Why** do you bargain for/negotiate the prices? 講價原因

purchase in bulk/in large quantities / pay in cash / sign long-term contract

Step 4　**What** do you counter offer? 講價金額

10% off the offered price

Outline 這樣擬

寫信目的	開場感謝對方報價，但希望能再議價。
討價還價	說明希望爭取更多折扣及優惠服務。
懇請回覆	要求對方回覆確認報價，希望對方提供優惠。
信　　尾	客套語＋署名。

Dear Ms. Cooper,

We acknowledge receiving your quotations and samples of all your lines of beverages. We appreciate your prompt response.

In reply to your offer, we think the prices are higher than expected. We'd like to know if you can make some allowance, say 10% on the quoted prices of all the drinks available, considering we will make purchase in large quantities each semester, and that our term of payment is in cash.

We sincerely hope to build a long-term business relationship with you as our permanent drink supplier, and we intend to sign a long-term contract if you can consider our counter-offer favorably and let us have your acceptance.

I am looking forward to hearing from you soon.

Yours sincerely,
Bruce Wills

主題 2

中文翻譯

Cooper小姐您好：

我們已收到您所有系列飲料的報價和樣品。我們很感謝您即刻的回覆。

回應您的報價，我們覺得報價高於預期。我們想詢問您是否可以調降價格，給我們約報價10%的折扣，考慮到我們每學期都會大量訂購，以及考量到我們都以現金付款。

我們竭誠希望能和您建立長久的合作關係，讓您成為我們長期的飲料供應商，若您能考慮並接受我們的議價，我們甚至會計畫要和您簽訂長期合約。

期待盡快收到您的回覆。

Bruce Wills敬上

關鍵單字片語

1. **acknowledge** *v.* 告知收到

   I acknowledge receipt of her email.

   我有收到她的電子郵件。

2. **offer** *n.* 報價

   Thank you for making an offer, but we've found it too high to accept.

   謝謝您迅速報價,但我們覺得報價金額過高無法接受。

3. **make some/an allowance** 打折

   That store makes an allowance of 10% for cash payment.

   這家商店對於現金付款再折價10%。

4. **quoted** *adj.* 報價的

   We don't find the quoted prices competitive at all.

   我們不覺得您的報價有任何競爭力。

5. **relationship** *n.* 關係 (+ with)

   It's very important to maintain stable relationship with your suppliers.

   和供應商保持穩定的關係很重要。

6. **permanent** *adj.* 永久的;長期的

   You are offered an permanent position as a construction site supervisor.

   你得到了一個長期工地監工的職務。

主題 2

給力句型解說 👆

比較級 than expected　比預期來的…

My telephone bill is higher than expected.
我的電信帳單金額比我預期來的高。

句型觀念：

比較級 than + 形容詞

You've got more than necessary.
你已經擁有比所必需的多很多。

He has performed better than anticipated.
他比預期的表現好很多。

intend to V.　計畫打算去做

The entrepreneur intends to merger another company.
這位企業家計畫要併購另一家公司。

延伸句型：

1. **attempt to V. 企圖去做**
   The criminal attempted to escape the prison but failed.
   這名罪犯企圖越獄但卻失敗了。

2. **plan to V. 計畫去做**
   I have planned to go on working holiday in Australia this summer.
   我計畫今年暑假去澳洲度假打工。

換個對象寫寫看

Dear **Ms. Huckings**,
Thank you for your prompt quotations of printers in response to our enquiry.

However, we very much regret to tell you that we don't find the quoted price acceptable. **We have obtained offers from other suppliers and all of them made more attractive offers. Since we will make bulk purchase of 50 printers, we expect more competitive prices from you. We were wondering if you could reduce the prices by 15%, so you stand better chance of concluding the business.**

We sincerely hope to build a long-term business relationship with you if you can consider our counter-offer favorably and let us have your acceptance a.s.a.p.

Your prompt response will be much appreciated.

Sincerely,
Henry Millers

Huckings小姐您好：
感謝您迅速針對我們印表機的詢價作報價。

主題 2

但很遺憾的，我們無法接受您的報價。我們有其他廠商的報價，價格都比您的來的有吸引力。既然我們會大量採購50台印表機，我們期待能從您這裡取得更有競爭力的報價。我們想詢問您是否可以調降價格**15%**，以便有更多機會可以成交。

若您能考慮並接受我們的議價，並盡速回應答應我們的提議，我們竭誠希望能和您建立長久的合作關係。

若您能盡快回覆，將感激不盡。

Henry Millers敬上

好用句型大補湯

對方報價比市場或比其他議價者高

We very much regret to state we consider the prices out of line with the prevailing market level. Your quoted prices appear to be higher compared to those offered by other suppliers and we have other offers of similar items with much lower prices. To have the business concluded, we suggest the price be lowered by at least 10%.

我們很遺憾要告知您，我們覺得您的報價高於市場水準。您的報價和其他供應商的報價比起來也過高。我們得到的其他報價都比您的低很多。若要成交，我們建議您能降價至少10%。

對方報價讓自己沒有利潤空間

We would like to take this opportunity to cooperate with you. However, the quoted prices are way too high, which will leave no margin of profit on our side, and it will be rather difficult to push any sales if we accept the prices as quoted. Could you please cut the prices by 10% so as to enable us to introduce your products to more customers?

我們很想利用這個機會和您合作。但您的報價過高,這會讓我們沒有利潤空間。若我們接受這個報價,將難以帶動銷售量。您是否可以給個10%的折扣,讓我們可以介紹您的產品給更多顧客?

其他議價的萬用句型:

1. I'm afraid that your quoted prices are too high and thus we find it difficult to accept the offer.
   我們認為您的報價太高,因此我們難以接受。

2. We think we are eligible to obtain a substantial discount to your quoted price, considering we'll make bulk purchase.
   我們認為我們有資格要求更多的折扣,考慮到我們會大宗採購。

3. If you can quote us a 10% discount off your list price, we would very much appreciate.
   若您能依報價打個10%折扣給我們,我們將感激不盡。

主題 2

Unit
06 詢問規格

寫作策略

Step **1** **Who** are you writing to? 你要寫給誰？

Mr. Josh Thomas

Step **2** **What** products are you interested in purchasing?
你有興趣購買什麼產品？

standard twin bed, mattress & quilt

Step **3** **What** is the purpose of this email?
這封email的目的什麼？

asking the measurement of the furniture

Outline 這樣擬

寫信目的	開場自我介紹，點出對該公司產品有興趣，想要詢價。
請教細節	請對方具體報價，提供商品價格、數量、規格、單位、裝船貨運時間、付款方式等細節。
懇請回覆	要求對方回覆確認報價，希望對方提供優惠。
信　　尾	客套語＋署名。

看看老師怎麼寫 🌏

To Mr. Josh Thomas,

I am looking for a bed, mattress, and comforter for my bedroom. I am very interested in the standard twin bed (No. TL525) and its matching mattress and quilt listed on your online furniture catalog. But I have a few questions regarding the measurements of the furniture.

I'd like to know the dimensions of the bed and mattress. As for the comforter, I am over 5'8" inches tall. I expect nothing smaller than a full five feet wide and 80 inches in length.

Please provide detailed measurements about the above items. Thank you and I look forward to hearing from you.

Sincerely,
Bobby Lincecum

主題 2

中文翻譯 ✍

Josh Thomas先生您好：
我正在為我的臥室尋找床組（床架，床墊和棉被）。我對你們網站型錄上的標準單人床（編號TL525）以及配套的床墊和棉被很感興趣，但我對於尺寸有些疑問。

我想要知道床架和床墊的尺寸，至於棉被的部分，我身高超過5英尺8吋，我想要找的棉被大小不能小於5英尺寬和80英吋長。

請提供上述物件詳細的尺寸。

謝謝您，期待您的回覆。

Bobby Lincecum敬上

關鍵單字片語

1. **standard** *n.* 標準；規格 *adj.* 標準的
   Searching luggage at airports is now standard practice.
   檢查行李已經是機場的標準執行步驟。

2. **measurements** *n.* 尺寸（必用複數型）
   Take measurements of the room before you buy any new furniture.
   在買新家具之前，要先丈量屋子的大小。
   measure *v.*

3. **dimensions** *n.* 尺寸（長寬高）
   What are the dimensions of the TV set?
   這台電視的尺寸為何？

4. **inch** *n.* 英吋
   He just bought a flat TV which is 24-inch wide.
   他剛買了一部24吋寬的電視。

5. **foot** *n.* 英尺
   This giant penguin stands almost 4 feet and 5 inches tall.
   這隻巨大的企鵝站著將近有4英尺5英吋高。

6. **wide** *adj.*　寬的 (=offer, provide)

How wide is the door? It's almost 2 feet wide.

這扇門有多寬？約莫兩英尺寬。

給力句型解說 👉

度量單位形容詞用法

物品 + is + 數字 + 度量單位 + long/wide/deep/thick/tall/ high

The table is two meters long.

這張桌子有兩公尺長。

The pond is eighty centimeters deep.

這個池塘有八十公分深。

The mountain is two miles high.

這座山有兩英里高。

The basketball player is two meters tall.

這位籃球選手有兩公尺高。

How much do/does + S + weigh (v.) +數字 + 度量單位

How much does this tablet computer weigh? It weighs 1 kilogram.

這個平板電腦有多重？一公斤重。

物品 + is + 數字 + 度量單位 + in + length, width, depth, height, weight

The table is two meters long. =The table is two meters in length.

這張桌子有兩公尺長。

The pond is eighty centimeters deep. =The pond is eighty

主題 2

109

centimeters in depth.

這個池塘有八十公分深。

The mountain is two miles high. =The mountain is two miles in height.

這座山有兩英里高。

What is the + length, width, depth, height, weight + of + 物品?

How wide is the table? =What's the width of the table?

這張桌子有多長？

How deep is the pond? =What's the depth of the pond?

這個池塘有多深？

換個對象寫寫看

To **Mr. Richardson**,

I am looking for a refrigerator for my kitchen. **I am very interested in your award winning Domestic Refrigerator (CR-1051) listed on your online furniture catalog. But I have a few questions regarding the measurements and features.**

I'd like to know the dimensions of the refrigerator. Besides, can you tell me the details of the features? I was also wondering how many colors to choose from.

Thank you and I look forward to hearing from you.

Sincerely,
Claire Lee

Richardson先生您好：

我正在為我的廚房尋找冰箱。我對你們網站型錄上有得獎的家用冰箱(編號
CR-1051)感興趣。但我對於尺寸和性能有些疑問。

我想要知道冰箱的尺寸，此外也請您告訴我詳細的性能。我也想知道我有多
少有少顏色可以選擇。

謝謝您，期待您的回覆。

Claire 李　敬上

好用句型大補湯

產品規格

Please send me the product specifications of Dell Optiplex 700 tablet. I'd like to know about the size, including height, width, depth, and weight.

請提供Dell 型號Optiplex 700平板電腦的產品介紹。我想知道尺寸相關的規格，包含高度、寬度、厚度以及重量。

產品性能

I'd like to know about the product features of the new i-Pad. Please provide the details for its storage capacity, and features of its display, cameras, photos, and video recording. I'm very curious about its operating system and system requirements.

我想知道新i-Pad的產品性能。請提供以下細節：記憶體容量以及顯示器、照相功能、錄影功能的性能。我也很好奇它所使用的操作系統以及系統需求。

其他詢問產品規格的的句型：

1. Please provide the product description details of model _____.

   請提供型號_____的產品說明細節。

2. I'd like to know more about features of your digital camera model _____.

   我想要知道更多有關數位相機型號_____的產品性能。

3. We would highly appreciate if you can forward the product description and specification of your TG LED(4W).

若您能附上TG LED(4W)的產品說明與規格細節，我們將非常感激。

4. Full / Detailed information regarding carton size and cubic capacity would be very appreciated.

若能詳列外箱子尺寸和裝櫃數量，將會讓我十分感激。

MEMO

主題 2

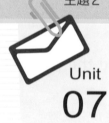

Unit
07
約定交貨

寫作策略 AB

Step 1　**Who** are you writing to?
這封信寫給誰？

Ms. Eileen Cooper

Step 2　**What** is the purpose of this email?
這封email的目的是什麼？

the delivery date of the order

Step 3　**What** did you order?
你訂了什麼？

printers, ink cartridge, A4 paper

Step 4　**When** did you order the goods?
你什麼時候訂的？

On October 19th

Step 5　**When** do you want the ordered goods to be delivered?
你希望的到貨時間？

October 25th

Outline 這樣擬

寫信目的　開場簡述訂單內容。

約定交貨時間　提出希望收到貨品的日期與時間。

懇請回覆　要求對方回覆確認可否配合。

信　　尾　客套語＋署名。

看看老師怎麼寫

Dear Ms. Cooper,

I'm writing this email concerning the delivery time of my order made on October 19th (Order No. 6520), which includes:

2 laser printers

5 ink cartridge

10 reams of A4 paper (white)

I'd like to know how long it usually takes for the goods to be delivered. I hope we can receive the ordered items by October 25th. Please confirm if our order can arrive by then.

Looking forward to hearing from you soon!

Yours sincerely,

Candy Jones

主題 2

中文翻譯

Cooper小姐您好：

我寫這封信是要問有關於我在10月19日所下的訂單（訂單號碼6520）的交貨時間。訂購商品包含：

2台雷射印表機

5個墨水匣

10包A4用紙（白色）

我想知道通常你們送貨要花多久時間。我希望我們可以在10月25日前收到訂購的品項。請您回覆我們的商品是否可以在那之前送達。

期待盡快收到您的回覆。

Candy Jones敬上

關鍵單字片語

1. **concerning** *adj.* 關於… (=about)

   I'm writing this email concerning the delivery date of my order.

   我寫信來詢問有關我的訂單交貨時間。

2. **laser** *n.* 雷射

   The laser eye surgery has both benefits and possible risks.

   雷射眼睛手術有其好處和可能的風險。

3. **printer** *n.* 印表機

   Most customers prefer color-laser printers to inkjet printers.

大部分的顧客喜愛彩色雷射印表機勝過噴墨印表機。

4. **ink**　*n.*　墨水

There's no need to toss out your pen when ink runs dry. You can purchase ink to refill the pen.

當你的筆沒有墨水時不必丟掉。你可以買墨水來填充。

5. **cartridge**　*n.*　墨水匣；筆芯

Most suppliers instruct their customers to replace ink cartridge when the cartridge is still half of ink.

大部分供應商會叫客戶在墨水匣還在半滿狀態下更換墨水匣。

6. **ream**　*n.*　一令（紙張計數單位，為500或516張）

Our company just ordered 500 reams of copy A4 paper from the manufacturer directly.

我們公司剛和製造商直接下單購買500令的A4影印紙。

給力句型解說 👉

關係代名詞which/ that的用法

1. 取代同一句子內的先行詞「事/物/動物」，可以用**that**取代。

   I have lost the watch. My mom bought me the watch last year.

   → I have lost the watch which/that my mom bought me last year.

   我搞丟了我媽去年買給我的手錶。

   （which指的是句子前半段提到的the watch）

2. 取代逗點前的整個句子，不可以用**that** 取代，此處**which**是單數名詞，後面接單數動詞。

   I have lost the watch. It made Mom very angry.

主題 2

→ I have lost the watch, which makes Mom very angry.

我搞丟了手錶，這件事讓媽媽很生氣。

（which指的是逗點前整句話I lost the watch）

How long does it take ... / It takes ...

How long does it take sb. to V.? 某人花了多少時間做……？

How long does it take for the technician to fix the car?

維修人員修理這輛車要花多久時間？

It takes某人 + 時間 + to V.

It takes the mechanic 2 hours to fix the car.

維修人員修理這輛車要花兩小時。

換個對象寫寫看

Dear **Ms. Wills**,

I'm writing this email to request speed delivery of my order made on November 11th (Order No. 6520).

The items include:

2 x P-48C Cross Cut Shredder (Black)

200 x Correction Tape (Pack of 2)

100 x Rapid Correction Fluid

50 x Epson A4 Paper (White, 500 Sheets)

I know it usually takes 5 working days to make a delivery. **However, is there any possibility that you can speed deliver the**

above items by November 14th? We would much appreciate if you can help make the speed delivery.

Looking forward to your confirmation!

Yours sincerely,
Belly Silverstone

Wills小姐您好：

我寫這封信是要問我在11月11日所下的訂單（訂單號碼6520）可否以速件出貨。

訂購商品包含：

2台P-48C機型碎紙機（黑色）

200套修正帶（一套包含兩個）

100個修正液

50包Epson A4紙（白色，每包500張）

我知道通常你們送貨要花5個工作天。但你們是否有可能盡速出貨，在11月14日前送達該批訂單？

期待盡快收到您的回覆確認！

Belly Silverstone敬上

好用句型大補湯 📋

再次詢問交貨時間

The goods we ordered (No. 56250) on October 19th were supposed to arrive on October 23rd. But it's already October 25th and we still haven't received them yet. We'd like to know what caused the delay. And please notify when you will deliver the items.

我們在10月19日訂購的商品（訂單編號56250）原定應該在10月23日就送達了，但現在已經是10月25日，我們卻還沒收到。我們想了解為何送貨時間會拖延，也請通知你們何時會送貨。

希望對方比預定時間更早交貨

We'd like to request for express delivery of our order made on October 19th (Order No. 6520). It's originally scheduled to arrive on October 25th. However, is it possible that we can receive the goods by October 23rd? Please confirm if you can make the delivery and let us know if there's additional charge for express delivery.

我們很想請您盡快寄送我們在10月19日訂購的商品（訂單編號56250）。該訂單商品原本預定會在10月25日送達。但我們想問有可能可以在10月23日前收到這批物品嗎？請確認您們是否可以速件處理該訂單，也請讓我們知道你們是否要額外收取快速寄件的費用。

其他討論交貨時間的句型：

1. Could you tell us how long it is likely to take you to deliver the goods?
   可否請你們告知送貨可能要花多久時間？

2. We'd like to know when you can make the delivery of Order No._____.
   我們想知道你們何時可以寄出訂單編號_____的商品。

3. We would much appreciate if the goods of our order No._____ can arrive by October 25th.
   若能在10月25日前收到訂單編號_____的商品，我們將十分感激。

4. I'd like to know if it's possible that we can receive the order No._____ by October 25th.
   我們想知道是否能在10月25日前收到訂單編號_____的貨品。

主題 2

Unit 08 確認交易

寫作策略 A B

Step 1　**Who** are you writing to? 對象

Mr. Michael Carrington

Step 2　**What** is this email for? 主旨

relationship, cooperation

Step 3　**What** will the other party do for you? 對方為你做什麼？

to cater for dinner party

Step 4　**Details** of the work/project 工作細節

menu, schedule

Outline 這樣擬

寫信目的	開場感謝對方與您合作。
細節確認	條列出合作內容，具體提供細節。
懇請回覆	要求對方回覆確認，期待雙方合作愉快。
信　　尾	客套語＋署名。

看看老師怎麼寫

Dear Mr. Carrington,

I enjoyed meeting you last Friday. Your enthusiasm for the menu for our Dec. 13th dinner party in the Redwood is contagious. My mouth is already watering!

According to my notes, you will be preparing the following for our 87 valuable guests:

Main course: Choice of chicken picata or vegetarian Medley Plus

Salad: Frensh spinach, mandarin orange, and almond salad

Appetizer: Angel hair pasta with white clam sauce

Dessert: Raspberry and white chocolate tarts

Drink: Coffee or herbal tea

Also, your staff of ten will arrive at 4:30 p.m. for set up, serve the food at 7 p.m. and handle the clean-up. The dinner will end no later than 10 p.m.

Please confirm the above details and don't hesitate to contact me for any further questions.

Look forward to your high-quality dining services.

Yours truly,
Trudy Jolie

主題 2

中文翻譯

Carrington先生您好：

很高興上週五和您會面。您為12月13日在紅木廳辦的晚宴設計菜單，您的熱情很有渲染力，我早就口水直流了。

根據我的筆記，您會我們87位嘉賓準備以下佳餚：

主菜：雞肉捲餅或綜合蔬食。
再加上
莎拉：新鮮菠菜佐金桔杏仁莎拉
前菜：天使義大利細麵佐蛤蜊白醬
甜點：覆盆子白巧克力塔
飲料：咖啡或花草茶

此外，您的十人團隊會在4點半就開始佈置會場，七點開始上餐，並處理後續的清潔與整理。晚宴會在十點前結束。
請確認以上細節，有任何疑問歡迎請與我聯繫。

期待享受您高品質的餐飲服務。

Trudy Jolie敬上

關鍵單字片語

1. **notes** *n.* 筆記;紀錄 (= records)

   The diligent student takes notes of every lecture he attends.

   這名用功的學生每場講堂都會抄筆記。

2. **valuable** *adj.* 有價值的

   This vase is valuable due to its unique designs.

   這個花瓶因為它獨一無二的設計而價值非凡。

3. **appetizer** *n.* 開胃菜

   What's the appetizer for today's set?

   今日套餐的開胃菜是什麼?

4. **set up** 準備

   The chef and his staff got up early to set up for the brunch.

   主廚和他的團隊起個大早準備早午餐。

5. **handle** *v.* 處理

   This experienced counselor can handle challenging interpersonal issues.

   這位經驗豐富的諮詢師可以處理極具挑戰性的人際相處課題。

6. **clean up** 打掃清理

   Mom enjoys the process of cooking but is not that into clean up.

   媽咪很享受煮飯的過程但不是很喜歡清理。

主題 2

給力句型解說 👆

enjoy + V-ing　喜歡去做……

He enjoys listening to Korean pop songs.
他喜歡聽韓國流行音樂。

延伸句型：

like /love + to V/V-ing

Jenny likes to play the piano. = Jenny likes playing the piano.
Jenny喜歡彈鋼琴。

be into + V-ing/N.

He is into watching soap opera.
他很喜歡看連續劇。

be fond of V-ing

He is fond of sharing photos on Facebook.
他喜歡在臉書上分享照片。

prepare (O.) for N.　為……準備……

Mom is preparing dishes for the dinner party.
媽咪正在為晚宴準備菜餚。

句型觀念：

prepare for N.　為……作準備

He is preparing for the college entrance exam.

他正在準備大學入學考試。

prepare oneself for N. 為……作好準備
You need to prepare yourself for the strict training.
你要為這個嚴格的訓練做好準備。

MEMO

換個對象寫寫看

Dear **Ms. Lee,**

I'm so delighted to have such an experienced wedding planner as you help me put together the most important event in my life, my wedding ceremony scheduled on Sun. December 19th. I enjoyed meeting with you last Friday discussing the outlines for the wedding of my dream!

According to the contract we signed when we met, you will be preparing the following details two months ahead of the ceremony:

- Compile guest's list, and update their contact information
- Order invitation cards and cake coupons
- Choose gifts for wedding party
- Discuss menu requirement with party venue, or better yet, arrange a tasting dinner
- Discuss venue setup specifications with hotel
- Try out makeup and hairstyle
- Confirm transportation arrangements
- Finalize seating plan

Please confirm the above details and I'd like to schedule further meetings for my hairdo and venue setup.
Looking forward to your counseling.

Yours truly,
Bella Whitman

李小姐您好：
很高興能請到像您這樣經驗豐富的婚禮策劃高手為我打造我這一生最重要的場合，我的婚禮（預定在12月19日舉辦）。我很開心上週五和您見面討論我夢想中的婚禮的雛型。

根據我們見面當天簽訂的合約，您會在婚禮前兩個月完成以下事項：
‧確認賓客名單和連絡資料
‧發婚宴邀請卡和伴手禮卡
‧挑選婚禮派對的禮物
‧和會場討論餐宴需求，並安排婚宴菜餚試吃
‧和會場討論佈置細節
‧試化新娘妝和髮型
‧確認當天禮車以及交通安排
‧確認賓客座位

請確認以上細節。此外我也想跟您敲定後續和您見面的時間，以進一步討論新娘裝扮和場地場佈的時間。
期待您提供諮詢。

Bella Whitman敬上

主題 2

好用句型大補湯

表達感謝對方給予合作機會

1. We are very delighted to have finally built business partnership with you.

   我們很開心終於和您建立了合作關係。

2. Thank you for the opportunity to offer you high-quality products/services. We'll definitely do our best to exceed your expectations.

   謝謝您給我們機會讓我們提供您高品質的產品或服務。我們定當全力以赴以超越您對我們的期待。

3. I'd like to take this opportunity to express our gratitude of being at your service with our fantastic products/services.

   我想藉這個機會表達感謝之意，感謝您讓我們為您服務，提供您高品質的產品與服務。

提供合作細節請對方確認

1. I have enclosed the notes / contract for all the details of the project. Would you please take some time to look into the terms or conditions of the contract and reply this email to confirm or report any changes or questions.

   我附上這個企劃案的細節／合約。請您花些時間過目所有條款或細節，並回覆確認或是回報任何您想做的修正或發現的問題。

2. I have summarized all the details of our corporation in this project and please refer to the enclosed notes. It would be appreciated if you can read them thoroughly to confirm that you agree with all the terms and details.

我已經摘要所有合作細節，請看附件我的摘要紀錄。若您能詳細過目並確認同意所有條約和細節，我將感激不盡。

3. Enclosed please read the details of responsibilities for both parties regarding the business partnership. Your confirmation of all matters will be much appreciated and please don't hesitate to point out any questions for further discussion or clarification.

附件是我們雙方合作的工作細節。您若能確認所有細項，定當感激不盡。也請不吝提出任何疑問，以便進一步討論或澄清。

重申本公司會遵守工作合約

1. We will comply to all the terms and conditions listed in the contract.

我們會遵守合約所有規定與條件。

2. We will abide by all regulations and fulfill all the responsibilities we both agree with.

我們會遵守所有規定並完成我們共同同意的工作內容。

主題 2

Unit
09
詢問發票

寫作策略 AB

Step **1** **Who** are you writing to?
你要寫給誰？
Mr. Curt Lee

Step **2** What is the **purpose** of this email?
這封email的目的是什麼？
asking details of the receipt

Step **3** the **information** shown on the receipt
發票上的資訊
receipt number, buyer's name, Unified Business No.

Outline 這樣擬

寫信目的	開場說明訂單已收到貨款和出貨事宜。
發票細節	請教對方發票上是否要附上抬頭或統編。
懇請回覆	要求對方回覆確認。
信　　尾	客套語＋署名。

看看老師怎麼寫 🌐

Dear Mr. Lee,

Thank you so much for shopping (Order No. 84512) through our website. We received your payment of NT$12,500 **via money order** on November 12th. The goods will be shipped tomorrow along with the **receipt**, and the **package is supposed to** be delivered by November 17th.

We have one question regarding the receipt. Would you like to include the **name/title of the addressee** and **Business Registration Code** or **Unified Business Number**?
Looking forward to your reply regarding the receipt today!

Sincerely,
Andria Tseng

主題 2

中文翻譯

李先生您好：

謝謝您透過我們網站購物（訂單編號84512）。我們已經在11月12日收到貨款台幣12,500元的匯票。商品明天會連同發票一起出貨，包裹將於11月17日前送達。

我們有個關於發票的疑問。您希望我們在發票上註明收據抬頭以及營業登記號碼／統一編號嗎？

期待您能今天回覆！

Andria 曾 敬上

關鍵單字片語

1. **money order** 匯票

   I'm about to cash the money order at the bank.

   我等一下要去銀行將匯票兌現。

2. **receipt** *n.* 收據

   Fill out the information on the sales receipt, tear off one copy for your customer and keep a copy for your business records.

   填好收據後，撕下收執聯給客戶，商家自己保留存根聯記帳用。

3. **package** *n.* 包裹

   My package arrived safely without any cracks the day after I paid it.

   我的包裹在我付款一天後就送達了，完好無缺損。

4. **name/title of the address** 收據抬頭

   I'd like to include the name of the address on my receipt, in order to be reimbursed for business expenses.

   我想要在收據上註明抬頭，以便回公司報公帳。

5. **Business Registration Number** 營業註冊登記編號

   The public can enquire the business registration number of a business.

   一般大眾可以查詢一家企業的營業登記證。

6. **Unified Business Number** 統一編號 (= Business Registration Code / Company Tax ID /Unified Business Identifier (UBI) number)

   You need to fill in Business License application to obtain the Unified Business Number for your company.

   你要填寫營利事業登記申請，以替你的公司取得統一編號。

給力句型解說

via + N. 透過（以…方式）

You can access our homepage via the Internet.
你可以透過網路連結到我們的網站。

延伸句型：

1. **through** 透過；穿透

   She got her first job through an employment agency.
   她透過求職仲介找到第一份工作。

   I can see through the curtains.

主題 2

我可以透過窗簾看到後面的景物。

2. **by + V-ing 藉由做…**

I apologized to her by sending a text message.

我用傳簡訊的方式向她道歉。

3. **by means of + N. 藉由…方式**

I escaped by means of a secret tunnel.

我從一個秘密通道逃走了。

4. **with + N.**

Please chop the onions with a sharp knife.

請用這把鋒利的刀切洋蔥。

be supposed to V.　應該會

1. 搭配被動語態：**be supposed to be p.p.**

This parcel is supposed to be shipped by Friday.

這包裹應該在週五前被寄達。

2. 不定詞搭配被動語態：**to be p.p.**

He doesn't want to be eliminated from the competition.

他不想從比賽中被淘汰。

The scandal of this government official has to be revealed to the public.

這名官員的醜聞必須被揭發。

換個對象寫寫看

Dear **Ms. Lin**,

Thank you so much for purchasing cosmetics and skin care products (Order No. 84512) through Beauty Buy.com. **We received your payment of NT$8990 via ATM on Feb 15th. The goods will be shipped tomorrow along with the receipt, and the package is supposed to arrive by Feb 20th.**

As for the receipt, would you like the name/title of the addressee and Unified Business Number to be shown on the receipt?

Your prompt reply would be much appreciated.

Sincerely,
Andy Chang

林小姐您好：

謝謝您透過Beauty Buy.com網站購買化妝品和保養品（訂單編號84512）。我們已經在**2月15日**收到您**ATM**轉帳貨款台幣**8990**元。商品明天會連同發票一起出貨，您應該會在**2月20日**前收到包裹。

至於發票，您希望我們在發票上註明收據抬頭以及統一編號嗎？

您若能盡速回覆，我們將十分感激。

Andy 張 敬上

主題 2

好用句型大補湯

Invoice 請款單

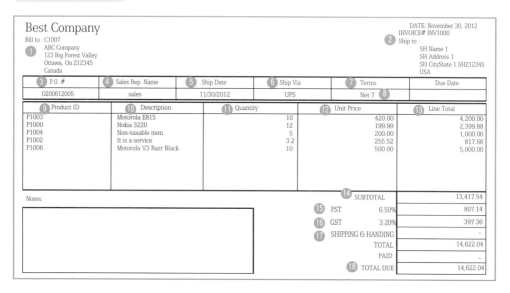

① bill to 帳單寄送地址

② ship to 收貨地址

③ P.O. # = purchase order number 訂單編號

④ Sales Rep. Name=Sales Representative Name 銷售員姓名

⑤ ship date 出貨時間

⑥ ship via 送貨方式

⑦ terms 付款方式

⑧ Net 7 請在請款單開立後7天內付款

⑨ product ID 商品代號

⑩ description 品項說明

⑪ quantity 數量

⑫ unit price 商品單價

⑬ line total 單品項總金額

⑭ subtotal 小計

⑮ PST (Provincial Sales Tax) 地方省府課徵的消費稅

⑯ GST (Goods and Services Tax) 消費與服務稅

⑰ shipping and handling 運費和服務費

⑱ total due 請款總金額

Receipt 收據

RECEIPT			
Date ____ / ____ / ____		Number _____	
Received from _____		$ _____	
		Dollars	
For Payment of _____			
From _____ To _____			
⑲ Amount Due		☐ Cash	
⑳ Amt Paid		☐ Check㉒　㉓ Check No. ____	
		☐ Money Order　Money Order No. ____	
㉑ Balance		☐ Credit Card	
Memo _____		By _____	

⑲ amount due 應繳金額

⑳ amt paid (amount paid) 已繳金額

㉑ balance 餘額 (尚須繳納的金額)

㉒ check 支票

㉓ money order 匯票

主題3　公關客服不馬虎！

Unit 01 發布活動消息

寫作策略

Step 1　**Who** are you writing to? 對象

Mr. Johnson Lee

Step 2　**What** is this email for? 主旨

event announcement

Step 3　**What** is the event? 活動

regular sale

Step 4　**What** kind of store is having the sale? 出售商品

furniture

Step 5　**Information** of the event 資訊

address, date

Outline 這樣擬

寫信目的	開場宣布活動主旨。
活動細節	具體說明時間地點和相關細節。
懇請光臨	懇請對方蒞臨參與。
信　　尾	客套語＋署名。

看看老師怎麼寫

Dear Mr. Lee,

Great Furnishings is proud to announce the beginning of our year-end furniture clearance sale!

From November 1st to 14th 2013, everything in our showroom will be marked down at least 50%! Nowhere else in town will you find better deals on the greatest chairs, sofas, closets, and other household furnishings. On the last day of the sale, receive an additional 10% off everything in our store.

Our entire inventory must go! Come visit us at 352 Pine Road, Da-An District, Taipei City, and pick up some great furniture at unbeatable prices!

Sincerely,
Great Furnishings

主題 3

李先生您好：

Great家具家飾店很驕傲宣布年終清倉大拍賣要開始囉！

從2013年11月1日到14日，展示間的所有家具起標價下殺至少5折。您不可能在城內其他地方找到更好的價格，購買品質最棒的椅子、沙發、衣櫥和其他居家家飾用品。

活動最後一天，所有家具享有額外10%的折扣。

我們要清空所有現貨。快來台北市大安區松樹路352號，以無可比擬的超低價購買最棒的家具。

Great家具家飾店敬上

關鍵單字片語

1. **year-end clearance sale** 年終清倉大拍賣
   Customers are long awaiting the year-end clearance sale for deeply-discounted items.
   顧客都在等年終清倉大拍賣，為了折扣殺很大的商品。

2. **showroom** *n.* 展示間；展場；陳列室
   The showroom presents the microphones in different recording situations.
   陳列室中展示針對不同收音情境設計的麥克風。

3. **furniture** *n.* 家具
   This sofa is the most expensive piece of furniture in our house.
   這件沙發是我們家裡所有家具中最貴的。

4. **deal** *n.* 交易
   You can get the best deal at our anniversary sale.
   您可以在我們週年慶上獲得最划算的交易。

5. **household** *adj.* 家庭的
   There are lots of household appliances to choose from at this electronic store.
   在這間電器賣場裡有很多家電用品可以選購。

6. **inventory** *n.* 庫存
   The retailer reduces its inventory by having a big sale.
   這間零售商以大拍賣出清他的庫存。

主題 3

給力句型解說 👍

否定副詞＋主要子句，以倒裝句型呈現

否定副詞：never, nor, neither, not only, not until

部分否定：　rarely, hardly, barely scarcely, seldom

表示少量：little, few, only

倒裝句型：類似問句句型，**Be**動詞或助動詞提到主詞之前

Nowhere else in town will you find better deals on the greatest furniture.

= You will not find better deals anywhere in town....

你不會在城裡其他地方以更好的價格買到最棒的家具。

延伸句型概念：

1. **Never + 倒裝句　從未；決不**

   Never will I forgive him. = I will never forgive him.

   我決不會原諒他。

2. **Not until .... + 倒裝句　一直到…才…**

   Not until one loses health will he realize the importance of it.

   要等到失去健康，才知道健康的重要。

   = He won't realize the importance of health until he loses it.

3. **Only ....+ 倒裝句　只有**

   Only when you lose health do you know the importance of it.

   = You know the importance of health only when you lose it.

   只有當失去健康，才知其重要性。

come + (and) 原型動詞　快來做…

Come (and) visit our new apartment.

快來參觀我們的新公寓。

1. 延伸句型：go + (and) 原型動詞　去做…

   Let's go (and) see the movie. 我們一起去看電影。

2. 比較句型：go + V-ing　娛樂或運動

   She goes shopping almost every weekend.

   她幾乎每週末去逛街購物。

換個對象寫寫看

To **Ms. Tsai**,

Please join Amazon for a press conference held on Thursday, September 6, at 10:00 a.m. at Ritz Taipei.

Amazon has unleashed new versions of our electronic book readers as well as revealed our first multimedia tablet. As the world's largest Internet store, we will update our Kindle and Kindle Fire lineups. Get ready to be impressed with the terrific features at the conference.

Get the first-hand information of our new lineup of e-book readers, tablets and have a glimpse onto our long-awaited smartphone!

Please reply this email to confirm participation to this press conference, so I can secure a seat for you. Feel free to contact me for further information and request for press packets.

主題 3

Sincerely yours,
Owen Swisher

蔡小姐您好：

歡迎您參加亞馬遜的記者會，時間是**9月6日**週四上午十點，在台北麗池酒店。

亞馬遜已經推出最新版的電子書，並且發表了我們第一款多媒體平板電腦。身為全世界最大網路商店，我們會更新我們的Kindle 和Kindle Fire系列商品，在記者發表會上您可以準備好見證其優越性能。快來取得第一手我們最新電子書、平板電腦和萬眾期盼的智慧型手機情報。

請回覆此信確認參加記者會，以便為您保留座位。歡迎與我聯繫取得更多資訊或取得媒體用說明手冊。

Owen Swisher 敬上

好用句型大補湯

促銷方案

Come visit us on November 14th for a special end-of-sale barbeque and live concert in the evening. At this party, present a receipt of any purchase amount at our sale and you'll get a free glass of cocktail! What are you waiting for? Join us for the fun and the drink by getting your house a nice piece of furniture at unbelievable prices.

歡迎蒞臨於11月4日晚上結束特賣烤肉聚會和現場演唱會。在派對上，只要您秀出一張在本拍賣購物的收據（金額不限）就可以享有一杯免費的雞尾酒。你還在等什麼呢？以無法置信的超值價為您的家增添一組好家具，順道加入我們玩樂一番並喝一杯。

活動需攜帶的物品

In appreciation of your regular patronage, we wish to extend our appreciation by sending you an invitation to attend a private sales of women's clothing at our department store on Friday, July 23rd starting 5:00 pm. Our regular patrons will have first selection on that day before the sale is open to the public. If you care to avail yourself of this special occasion, please bring this invitation letter with you and present it at our women's department.

為了感謝您常常光顧，我們寄出私人的邀請，歡迎您蒞臨7月23日下午五點開始，針對女裝部門辦的會員日封館特賣會。我們的常客可以在對一般大眾開放之前，優先挑選館內的服飾。如果您願意參與會員封館特賣，當天請攜帶本邀請函至女裝部門。

其他宣布活動訊息的萬用語

1. We enclose advance announcement of our Courtesy Day of Men's Suits and Shoes.
   我們附上活動通知函，優先通知您有關男裝和男鞋部門的會員特賣會訊息。

2. As one of our regular patrons, we're informing you with delight of the up-coming anniversary sale.
   您身為我們的常客，我們很高興通知您有關接下來的週年特賣訊息。

主題 3

149

Unit
02
舉辦餐會

寫作策略

Step 1　**Who** are you writing to? 對象

Ms. Witty Kao

Step 2　**What** is this email for? 主旨

ask attendees about their preferences or expectations of a dinner party

Step 3　**Questions** to ask the attendee 問題

Information, menu, dress, settings, RSVP

Outline 這樣擬

感謝參與餐會　開場感謝對方參與餐會，再次提醒餐會時間與地點。

需確認的細節　請教對方對於座位安排，餐點內容等要求或特殊喜好。

懇請回覆　要求對方回覆確認。

信　　尾　客套語＋署名。

看看老師怎麼寫 🌐

To Ms. Kao, Chairperson of Taipei City Women's Club,

Thank you for granting us with your presence to the dinner party we hold on 10th of June at 8 o' clock at Hotel Hayat. We would like to take this chance to display our latest apparel series to all our valued customers at the opening ceremony and hold a dinner party right afterwards. And we're honored to know that all the members of Taipei City Women's Club will attend this special occasion.

To make sure we can accommodate the needs of all our valued guests at the dinner party, we'd like to obtain as much information as possible about the dietary restrictions of our attendees. Your kind reply to the following inquiries would be highly appreciated:

The total number of guests (including family members):_____ adults _____children (7-12) _____children (under 6)
The number of guests who require vegetarian meals:
The number of guests who have special food limitations and details (e.g. don't eat beef, pork, or food allergies)

Please give us your confirmation by 29th of May.
Thank you again for your enthusiastic participation in the event and we are looking forward to attending to you.

Sincerely yours,
Douglas Jones

主題 3

151

中文翻譯

台北市婦女會主席 郭小姐您好：

謝謝您答應蒞臨我們6月10日晚上8點要在Hayat飯店舉辦的晚宴。我們將藉這個場合舉辦開幕典禮，為貴賓們展示我們最新的服飾系列，並隨即開始晚宴。我們很榮幸得知所有婦女會的成員都將蒞臨這個特殊的場合。

為了確定我們能照顧到所有晚宴貴賓的需求，我們想要收集詳盡的與會者對餐點的喜好資料。若您能回覆以下詢問，我們將不勝感激。
所有參與者人數（包含家族成員）：大人_____名，7-12歲兒童_____名，六歲以下幼兒_____名
點素食餐點者人數：
特殊飲食需求的人數以及細節（例如：不吃牛肉、豬肉或食物過敏）：

請您在5月29日前回覆。再次謝謝您熱情參與此盛會，期待為您服務。

Douglas Jones 敬上

關鍵單字片語

1. **opening ceremony**　開幕典禮
   The mayor is invited to cut the ribbon at the opening ceremony of a new shopping mall.
   市長受邀在一個新的購物商城的開幕典禮上剪綵。

2. **dietary** *adj.* 　和飲食相關的
This hospital cares for its patients' particular dietary needs.
這間醫院照顧病人的特殊飲食需求。

3. **restriction** *n.* 　限制
When planning meals or designing menus, it is important to enquire if the guests have any special food restrictions or allergies.
當計畫菜餚和設計菜單時，詢問賓客有無特殊食物不能吃或過敏是很重要的。

4. **attendee** *n.* 　與會者
The PR agent is helping its client to make the dinner attendee the list of its annual convention dinner.
這位公關公司的代表正在為他的客戶年度會員晚會製作與會賓客名單。

5. **vegetarian** *n.* 　素食者（口語: vegan）
Get delicious healthy vegetarian recipes for pasta from the chef at Hayat Hotel.
快來取得Hayat飯店主廚推出的好吃又健康的素食義大利麵食譜。

6. **allergy** *n.* 　過敏
Although most food allergies cause relatively mild and minor symptoms, some food allergies can cause severe reactions, and may even be life-threatening.
儘管大部分食物過敏導致輕微症狀，有些食物過敏會導致嚴重的反應，甚至有致命的可能。

主題 3

給力句型解說 👆

right + 地方或時間副詞 (right here / right now/right afterwards/ right in front of)

We will present a cat walk show and then a dinner party is held right afterwards.
我們會先以走秀展示呈現，隨即舉辦晚宴。
I'm running late for the class. I'm leaving right now.
我上課要遲到了，現在就得走。

延伸觀念：

1. **right** *adj.* 正確的 (=correct)
   His answer to this question is right.
   他這一題答案是正確的。
2. **right** *adj.* 右邊的 (左邊: left)
   Walk straight along this road for two blocks and turn left.
   沿這一條路走兩個街區再右轉。

attend to 　照料；照顧；服務；服侍 (=serve, take care of)

The waiter attends to 10 guests at the same time during the dinner hours.
這位服務生在晚餐時段一次服務10位客人。

延伸觀念：

1. **attend** *vt.* 參加
   The CEO himself will attend the shareholders' meeting.
   公司執行長會參加股東大會。

2. **attendee** *n.* 與會者

All attendees to the convention should wear identification badges.

所有年度代表大會的與會者都要佩戴識別證。

換個對象寫寫看

To **Mr. and Mrs. Paul Louis**,

On behalf of Taipei Lions Club, I'd like to express our sincere gratitude to your presence in our upcoming Sponsor Night on March 23rd at 6:30 p.m. at our Lions Hall for an evening full of great food, fellowship, and valuable information about Lions Club provided by our respected guest speaker, Mr. Vincent Wang.

To make sure we can attend to all our valued guests at the dinner, we'd like if you have any food requirements or allergies, so we can care for your dietary needs while you enjoy the good food, fun and some enlightenments on how you can serve your surrounding communities as well as around the world.

Please reply this email by March 10th as to the above inquiries. Thank you again for your enthusiastic participation in the event and we look forward to meeting you.

Sincerely,
Jill Manning

Paul Louis先生、夫人您好：

本人謹代表台北獅子會，感謝您蒞臨即將在3月23日舉辦的贊助之夜，晚會於6點半開始，地址在獅子會大樓，誠邀兩位共享一整晚的美食饗宴、聯誼，以及特別力邀貴賓Vincent Wang先生致詞介紹獅子會相關資訊。

為了確定我們能照顧到所有晚宴貴賓的需求，我們想知道您是否有任何飲食上的要求或食物過敏，好讓我們能照顧到您的飲食需求，讓您盡情享用美食、歡樂，以及得到啟發，了解您能如何貢獻所屬社區和全世界。

請您在3月10日前以郵件回答上述問題。
再次謝謝您熱情參與此盛會，期待與您見面。

Jill Manning敬上

好用句型大補湯

飲食特殊需求確認

We'd like your help to make this dinner party a successful event by providing your personal food limitations or requirements. Please feel free to notify us if you have any food allergies or limitations due to religions or health concerns, so we can provide personalized / specialized meals to accommodate your needs.

我們需要您提供您對飲食的限制或需求，讓這個餐會成功舉辦。若您對任何食物過敏，或因為宗教或健康考量不能吃特定食物，歡迎告知我們，以便為您提供符合您需求的個人餐點。

告知賓客餐宴的主題或特殊活動

Join us for the Christmas casino night, with cocktails and small plates. There will be a fancy dress competition and the best couple will be offered free special dinner for New Year's Eve at W Hotel. It's unofficially mandatory to help spread the spirit of Christmas for everyone who participates the competition.

請加入我們參加聖誕節賭博之夜，享受雞尾酒和小菜。現場也有豪華扮裝比賽，最佳扮裝的夫妻或情侶可以獲得免費除夕夜W飯店的晚餐。為了傳遞過聖誕的氣氛和精神，硬性規定每個人都要參加扮裝比賽。

其他邀約餐會的參考句型：

1. Black-tie is required. Hors d'oeuvres and Cocktails at 6:30p.m.. Dinner immediately following R.S.V.P. by October 25th.
   需著正式套裝。6點半點會先上冷盤和雞尾酒，隨即開始晚宴。請在10月25日前回覆是否出席。

2. Let us take the chance to invite all our sponsors and suppliers to our company's up-coming year-end dinner party 25th December. I, on behalf of our company, have organized a buffet banquet and lot-drawing party at our head office premises itself. We sincerely hope you enjoy the party with us all.
   讓我藉這個機會邀請所有我們公司的贊助商和合作廠商參與我們公司在12月25日舉辦的的年終晚會。我代表本公司策劃在本公司總部舉辦的自助餐和抽獎，期望您與我們一起同樂。

3. We will have both vegetarian and non-vegetarian dishes.
   我們會提供素食和非素食的菜單。

主題 3

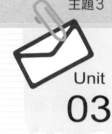

Unit
03
填寫回函

寫作策略

Step **1** **Who** are you writing to? 對象

participant

Step **2** **What** is the mail about? 主旨

post-event survey

Step **3** **What** is the event? 活動

a conference/ seminar/speech

Outline 這樣擬

[寫信目的] 開場說明自己參加特定活動，提供會後感想。

[感想與意見] 具體說明對活動各方面的感想。

[感 謝] 感謝對方此活動，希望自己的意見能有所幫助。

[信 尾] 客套語＋署名。

看看老師怎麼寫

Dear Participant,

We would like to thank you for your participation in the conference.

The organizing committee would like to invite you to take a moment to complete our conference evaluation feedback. Your feedback will enable us to improve our conferences and better meet your needs.

This evaluation will take no more than 5 minutes of your time.

Thanks for your collaboration.

1. Please indicate your overall satisfaction with this conference:
   ☐Very satisfied　　　　　☐Somewhat satisfied
   ☐Neither satisfied nor dissatisfied
   ☐Somewhat dissatisfied　　☐Very dissatisfied
2. How would you rate the following items? (excellent/very good/good/fair/poor)
   (1) Relevance of conference contents
   (2) Providing a forum for exchange of information with other participants
   (3) Quality of presentations
3. What is the most valuable of the conference or any suggestions?

主題 3

We highly appreciate any of your comments, ideas, and suggestions. The email will be solely for the use of evaluating this event and the information you share will be confidential.

Sincerely,
Coast Organizing Committee

中文翻譯

與會者您好：

我們很感謝您參與本次會議！主辦單位想要請您花一些時間完成我們會議評鑑回饋表。您的回饋能讓我們會議越辦越好，且更能符合您的需求。

這份意見表不會花您超過5分鐘的時間，謝謝您的合作。

1. 請給予整體滿意度的評分：（很滿意/還算滿意/持平/些微不滿意/非常不滿意）

2. 請針對以下項目評分（傑出/很好/好/普通/不佳）

    (1) 會議內容的相關性

    (2) 提供和其他與會者交流的平台

    (3) 簡報的品質

3. 本次會議最有價值之處或您的建議。

我們很感謝您任何的評語、想法和建議。這封郵件將純粹用來評鑑本次活動品質，您所提供的資料將被保密。

Coast主辦單位 敬上

關鍵單字片語

1. **evaluation** *n.* 評鑑；考核

   They took some samples of products for evaluation.

   他們從產品中取樣作檢核。

2. **feedback** *n.* 回饋（+on）

   The teacher gave each student some feedback on their assignments.

   老師針對作業給予個別學生一些建言。

3. **collaboration** *n.* 合作 (= cooperation)

   You can get the best deal at our anniversary sale.

   您可以在我們週年慶上獲得最划算的交易。

4. **forum** *n.* 討論場所；交流平台 (=platform)

   The journal aims to provide a forum for discussion and debate.

   這個媒體雜誌目標為提供一個討論和辯論的交流平台。

5. **presentation** *n.* 簡報

   We will make a presentation to help the client fully understand our product.

   我們即將做簡報讓客戶了解我們的產品。

6. **confidential** *adj.* 機密的

   Doctors are required to keep patients' records completely confidential.

   醫生們被要求要將病患的病例資料保密。

主題 3

給力句型解說 👍

A enable B + to V　　A讓B能夠去做…

The loan enabled Jan to buy the house.
這筆貸款讓Jan可以買房子。

延伸句型：

1. **be able to V**　　有能力去做
   Jan is able to buy a house with the loan.
   因為有貸款，Jan能夠買房子。

2. **have the ability to V**　　有能力去做
   Jan has the ability to buy a house because she has got the loan.
   因為取得貸款，Jan有能力買房子。

3. **-able (adj.)** 複合形容詞以 "-able" 結尾，代表「可以…的」
   washable (=it can be washed) 可洗的
   unbreakable (=it cannot be broken) 摔不破的
   loveable (=easy to love) 可愛的

事物 + take + 人 + 時間 + to V(不加受詞)　　事物花某人…時間去…

This feedback form took me a minute to complete.
這份意見表花了我一分鐘時間完成。

It takes/took 人 + 時間 + to V(含受詞)

It took me a minute to complete this feedback form.

人 +spend + 時間 + on 名詞 / (in) Ving

I spent a minute completing the feedback form.
=I spent a minute on the feedback form.

換個對象寫寫看

Dear **Participants**,

We would like to thank you for your participation in the Fresh Career Workshop, which was aimed to prepare you for job interviews.

We'd like you to take a moment to complete our feedback survey, so we can improve the series of workshops. Thanks for your cooperation.

1. Please rate the following items by 1-5, 5 being the highest score:

Instructor Effectiveness:

The instructor has prepared well for the lesson.

The instructor is able to explain the points clearly.

The instructor is able to hold my interest.

The instructor interacts well with the class.

2. What do you think were the strengths of this course?

3. What could we do better?

We highly appreciate any of your comments, ideas, and suggestions. Thank you again for your participating to the event.

Sincerely,
Julie Brooms
Organizer of the workshop

與會者您好：

我們很感謝您參與本次職涯開展講座，此會議目的是讓您能準備工作的面試。

我們想請您花一些時間完成我們回饋意見調查表。您的回饋能讓我們這系列的講座越辦越好。謝謝您的合作。

1. 請針對以下項目以數字1到5評分（5為最高分）
   演講者的內容：
   演講者充分準備演講內容
   演講者將內容要點解釋清楚
   演講者讓我保持興趣和專注
   演講者和全班作互動
2. 本次講座成功之處:
3. 我們可以改進之處:

我們很感謝您任何的評語、想法和建議，再次謝謝您參與本活動。

主辦人
Julie Brooms敬上

好用句型大補湯

會議場地設備交通與飲食（硬體）

How did you find the catering?

您覺得我們提供的餐點供餐服務如何？

How do you like the conference venue/facilities?

您對於會議舉辦場地和設備意見如何？

What do you think about the dates of the conference?

您對於會議舉辦日期和時間滿意嗎?

How do you find the transportation/location of the venue (suitability of the venue)?

您對於會場的交通和位置意見如何（會場的合適度）？

其他詢問活動意見的問題：

1. We'd like to invite you to fill in the satisfaction questionnaires.
   我們想請您配合填寫活動滿意度調查問卷。

2. Would you recommend this event to others? (Definitely/ Not Sure/May not consider)
   您會推薦這個活動給其他人嗎？（一定會/不確定/可能不考慮）

3. Do you intend to attend next year's event? (Likely/Neutral/ Unlikely)
   你有意願想參加明年的會議嗎？（可能/持平/不太可能）

主題 3

Unit 04 貨物配送時間

寫作策略 A B

Step **1** **Who** are you writing to? 對象

Help Center Best Buy

Step **2** **What** do you want to know? 你想知道什麼？

When will my order be shipped?
When will my order arrive?

Step **3** Details of your **order** 訂單細節

name of items / special requirements

Outline 這樣擬

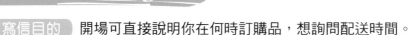

寫信目的 開場可直接說明你在何時訂購品，想詢問配送時間。

商品或配送細節 提醒對方你訂的商品內容或配送上的要求。

敬請回覆 要求對方回覆確認。

信 尾 客套語＋署名。

看看老師怎麼寫 🌐

Dear Sir / Ma'am,

My membership number is A02515. I am writing this letter to inquire the delivery status of my online order, tracking number Z1021.

I placed the order this morning and the goods included:
A freshly-baked chocolate birthday cake
A bouquet of 99 roses
I selected urgent delivery and I paid an extra NT$150 for shipping. I expect the order to arrive at my residential address within 1 business day.

I hope you can process my order promptly and reply to this inquiry a.s.a.p.
Thanks for your time.

Yours truthfully,
Jack Tseng

中文翻譯 ✉️

您好：

我的會員代號是A02515。我寫信是要詢問我的網路訂單寄送狀態。訂單代號是Z1021。

主題3

我今早訂的品項包含：

一個現做巧克力生日蛋糕

一束99朵玫瑰花束

我選擇急件快遞，也已額外付了台幣150元的運費。

我希望貨品能在一個工作天內送達我的住家地址。

希望您能盡速處理我的訂單並回覆以上詢問。

謝謝您的時間。

Jack 曾　敬上

關鍵單字片語

1. **order** *n.* 訂單

   I just placed an online order for office supply and the purchase amount totals $20,000.

   我才剛下了網路訂單訂辦公室用品，訂單金額合計2萬元。

2. **track** *v.* 追蹤；查詢

   The police have been tracking the four criminals all over central Taiwan.

   警方一直在整個中台灣追查這四名罪犯的下落。

3. **freshly-baked** *adj.* 剛出爐的

   Customers line up for the freshly-baked baguettes and croissants.

   顧客排隊為了搶買剛出爐的法式長棍麵包和丹麥麵包。

4. **bouquet** *n.* 花束

We brought our mom a bouquet of carnations on Mother's Day.

我們在母親節當天買給媽媽一束花。

5. **shipping**　*n.*　運送

If items are cancelled from an order and the order total falls below the minimum purchase amount for free shipping, then a shipping and handling fee will be applied to the remaining items.

如果刪除訂單上某些品項導致訂單金額低於免運費的門檻，則運費和手續費會被加在剩下的品項上。

6. **residential**　*adj.*　住宅的

The residential area and the commercial area are mixed in most cities in Taiwan.

台灣大多數城市裡住宅區和商業區是混合的。

給力句型解說

place an order　下訂單

It's easy to place an online order if you are already a member of this website.

若你已經是該網站的會員，在網路上下訂單很簡單。

place「動詞」的用法：放置

place an order 下訂單；**place an bid** 競標；**place an emphasis on** ...強調

Online shoppers can choose either to place a bid or purchase the item at a fixed price

網路買家可以選擇下標競價或是以定價購買商品。

S. + include + O.　包含

The items I have purchased on the website include accessories and cosmetics.

我在這網站上已購買過的商品包含飾品和化妝品。

延伸觀念：

include　v　, including　adj.　, included　adj　的用法：

1. include前面接S.（名詞）

   The nominees for Nobel Peace Prize include several workers for non-profit organizations.

   諾貝爾和平獎的被提名者包含了好幾位非營利組織的工作人員。

2. including為which include(s)的分詞片語，前面接句子和逗點，後面接名詞

   Many people are nomineed for the Nobel Peace Prize, including several NPOs workers / which includes several NPO workers.

3. included (adj.)為and ... is included的分詞片語，前面接句子和逗點，名詞則放在前面

   Many people are nomineed for the Nobel Peace Prize, several workers for NPOs included.

   = and several NPO workers are included.

換個對象寫寫看

Dear **Sir / Ma'am**,

My membership number is ZU3021. I am writing this letter to change the current recipient address for my order, tracking number PA2100.

I've checked the delivery status of the order with your staff and I've been informed it'll arrive before noon tomorrow. But since I won't be home to receive it, I'd like to get the order shipped to my work address as follows:

8F, No 32, Sec 3, Min-Chuang West Road, Taipei City

Please reply for confirmation of the above request.
Thanks for your time.

Yours truthfully,
Ben Ten

您好：

我的會員代號是ZU3021。我寫信是要更改我現在的送貨地址。訂單代號是 PA2100。

我剛和你們的人員查詢了目前送貨狀態，我已接獲通知商品會在明日中午前 送達。但因為我屆時不會在家，我想要本筆訂單改送到我的公司地址，地址 如下：

主題 3

台北市民權西路三段32號8樓

請回信確認收到以上要求。

謝謝您的時間。

Ben Ten　敬上

好用句型大補湯

詢問能否週六日送貨

I'd like to know more about your delivery policy. Once I place my order, can I demand it to be delivered on Saturdays or Sundays to places in Taipei City? / Are you able to do Saturday or Sunday deliveries?

我想要知道更多關於你們的送貨規定。一旦我下了訂單，我可以要求你們週六或週日運送到台北市內的地方嗎？你們是否接受週六日送件？

送貨時收件者不在家該如何處理？

The customer service staff says your couriers deliver is between 9.30am and 5.30pm. If I am not at home when you attempt to deliver, what will you do? Will the courier leave you with a calling card so I can rearrange the delivery for a more convenient day?

客服人員告訴我你們的送貨時間是早上9點半到下午5點半。如果你們要送貨時我不在家，你們會如何處理？送貨員會留給我他的電話號碼讓我跟他聯繫安排其他方便收件的日期嗎？

其他常問的網路購物疑問：

1. How can I check the information/ratings and reviews of the merchant/seller/retailer/store?
   我如何事先查看賣家的資料、評分與評價？

2. What is the minimum purchase amount for free shipping?
   免運費的最低消費金額為多少？

3. Will merchants ship their goods outside Taipei City?
   賣家是否能將他們貨品送至台北以外的縣市？

4. I'd like to make an alteration for the deliver address from my home address to my work address. How can I change/alter my billing and shipping information?
   我想把帳單和送貨地址作些改變，從住家改成我的公司地址。我該如何更改帳單地址或送貨地址？

主題 3

Unit
05

更改付費方式

寫作策略

Step **1** **Who** are you writing to? 對象？

Help Center Best Buy

Step **2** **What** do you request? 要求什麼？

change the payment method/option/preference

Step **3** **Payment** option 付款選擇

pay by installment

Outline 這樣擬

寫信目的 開場先給予訂單資料，並直接說明要更改付費方式。

細　節 更改付費方式的細節。

敬請回覆 要求對方收到訊息後回覆確認。

信　尾 客套語＋署名。

看看老師怎麼寫

Dear Sir,

I am writing to change the payment method for my latest order, Tracking Number TF2351. Instead of paying cash on delivery for the tablet, I'd like to pay by 4 installments by credit card with 0% interest.

I just noticed from your website about Pay Easy Installment Plan. It says that customers can spread the total purchase amount over several monthly payments with no interest. (Shipping and taxes will be added to the first payment.) The total value of my order is $399, so I will be charged with 4 monthly payments to my visa.

Please reply for confirmation of the above request.

Sincerely,
Julie Tseng

中文翻譯

您好：
我寫信來修改我最近一次的訂單（訂單索引號碼TF2351）。原本我選貨到付款，但我想改成分四期零利率刷卡付款。

我剛從你們網站上得知有關Pay Easy分期付款的方案。規定上說能將付款金

主題 3

額平均分攤成幾個月零利率（運費和貨物稅則會被加在第一期付款金額內）我的訂單總金額為美金399元，所以你們會以四期零利率向我的信用卡扣款。

請回覆確認以上要求。

Julie 曾　敬上

關鍵單字片語

1. **method**　*n.*　方式 (= way)

   An experienced teacher must master teaching methods.

   一位經驗豐富的老師一定專精教學方法。

2. **cash on delivery** 貨到付款

   Most customers without any bank account can choose to pay cash on delivery.

   大部分沒有銀行帳號的顧客可以選擇貨到付款。

3. **tablet**　*n.*　平板電腦（桌上電腦desktop　筆記型電腦laptop）

   This computer manufacturer just launched its latest model of tablets.

   這家電腦製造商剛推出一款平板電腦。

4. **installment**　*n.*　分期付款

   I'd like to pay for the jewelry by 6 installment.

   我想以6期分期付款購買珠寶。

5. **interest**　*n.*　利息；興趣

   The interest rate for mortgage is rising increasingly over the years.

貸款利率這幾年來不斷上升。

6. **tax**　*n.*　稅

He already pays 40% tax on his income.

他收入的4成都已拿去納稅。

給力句型解說

instead of + 名詞/V-ing　而不是

Since it is still raining outside, let's stay home **instead of going outside**.

既然還在下雨，我們待在家好了，不要外出。

You probably picked up my keys **instead of yours**.

你有可能拿了我的鑰匙，而不是你自己的。

延伸觀念：

比較instead和instead of

1. instead of後面接的 「N. / V-ing」是主詞沒有去做的事。

   Many young people download songs instead of purchasing CDs.

   很多年輕人下載音樂而不買CD。

2. instead前面接否定句子代表主詞沒做的選擇。後面先逗點，再接句子，代表主詞真正的選擇。

   Many young people don't buy CDs anymore. Instead, they download music.

主題 3

It (告示牌，規定) says that +子句 規定上寫說…

1. **It (a sign, rule, policy) says that + 名詞子句 告示牌/規定上寫說…**
   The sign says that there is no smoking in this area.
   告示牌上說此區域不可吸煙。

2. **It is said that + 名詞子句 據說…**
   It is said that this millionaire has devoted 80% of his fortune to charities.
   據說這位百萬富翁已經將8成財產捐給了慈善團體。

換個對象寫寫看

Dear Sir,

I am writing to change the payment method for my latest order, Tracking Number BM3521.

I'd like to choose ATM transactions for the amount of the order, instead of cash on delivery.

Since this order has exceeded 400 dollars, it's inconvenient for me to withdraw that much money in cash from my bank account. **I will transfer the total amount to your account no later than 2:00 pm tomorrow.**

Please reply for confirmation of the above request.

Sincerely,

Mandy Chou

您好：

我寫信來修改我最近一次的訂單的付款方式（訂單索引號碼**BM3521**）。

原本我選貨到付款，但我想改成**ATM**轉帳。

因為訂單金額超過400美元，要我從帳戶提領那麼多現金其實很不方便。

我會在明天下午兩點前將總金額匯到你的帳戶。

請回覆確認以上要求。

Mandy 邱　敬上

主題 3

好用句型大補湯

變更信用卡內容

I'd like to switch from visa to master card.

Card Holder's Name: Jeremy C. Chen

Card number: 4851 5214 9635 7458

Expiring Date: 2015/04/23

security number (the last 3 digits on reverse of card): 351

Please confirm receiving the updated credit card details.

我想從visa卡改成萬事達卡。

持卡人姓名：Jeremy C. Chen

卡號：4851 5214 9635 7458

失效日期：2015年4月23日

認證號碼（卡片背後末三碼）：351

請確認收到以上更新後的信用卡資訊。

其他更改付費方式常見的萬用語：

1. I'd like to alter my payment options from paying by cash to telegraphic transfer.

   我想要將付款選擇從現金付款改為電匯。

2. I'm writing this email to alter/update my payment method. I'd like to pay by TT when the shipment is ready.

   我寫信來更改/更新我的付費方式。我想要等貨物準備好後再電匯。

3. Please kindly help with my request for change of payment terms.

   煩請協助我變更付款方式。

4. I'd like to request to update my payment method. I will go with paying by check.

   我想要求變更付款方式。我會以支票付款。

MEMO

Unit
06

換貨

寫作策略 AB

Step 1 **Who** are you writing to? 對象？

customer service, Beauty Clothing Company

Step 2 **What** do you request? 要求什麼？

exchange for a product

Step 3 **What** do you ask for exchange of an item? 為什麼要換貨？

not fitting (size): too large/small/tight/loose/long/short

Outline 這樣擬

寫信目的	開場先給予訂單資料，並直接說明要求換貨。
細　　節	換貨原因和想要換的商品條件說明。
敬請回覆	要求對方收到訊息後回覆確認。
信　　尾	客套語＋署名。

看看老師怎麼寫 🌐

Dear Customer Service,

I am writing to ask for an exchange for the pair of linen trousers. I recently purchased by mail order, Order Number TF2351.

The pants included with this order are a 28 waist with a 34 length. Unfortunately, I need to exchange these for the same pants with a size of 24 waist and 32 length.

Please send someone to pick up the parcel. I'll enclose with this item a copy of the invoice and order number. I also understand there are no shipping charges added for making an exchange.

I would appreciate it if you could send the exchanged item to my home address.

Sincerely,
Isabella Freed

主題3

客服人員您好：

我寫信來要求更換我以郵購買的亞麻褲（訂單索引號碼TF2351）。
我訂單上買的褲子是腰圍28吋，長34吋。但很遺憾的是，我需要更換成腰圍24吋長32吋的同款式褲子。

請派人來收回包裹。我會附上發票影本和訂單編號。我知道我不必為換貨負擔運費。

若你們能將換好的商品送到我的住家地址，我將不勝感激。

Isabella Freed　敬上

關鍵單字片語

1. **trousers** *n.* 褲子 (= pants)
   He just spent NT$399 for a pair of designer jeans. What a bargain!
   他才剛花了台幣399元買了一條設計師款的牛仔褲。真是撿到便宜！
2. **mail order** 郵購
   She buys cosmetics and skin care products by mail order once a month.
   她每個月用郵購方式買化妝品和護膚產品。

3. **waist**　*n.*　腰部

The skirt was too big around the waist.

這件裙子在腰部的地方太寬大。

4. **length**　*n.*　長度

This ankle-length dress looks nice on Mary.

這件長度到腳踝的洋裝穿在Mary身上很好看。

5. **parcel**　*n.*　包裹 (= package)

The parcel was delivered last week and the recipient got it this morning.

這個包裹上週寄出，收件人今早拿到。

6. **invoice**　*n.*　發票；發貨單

Enclosed the package please find the invoice of all the items of this order.

包裹內附上這次訂購的所有物品的發票。

給力句型解說

exchange (n/v) for ...　　換成⋯

1. **exchange A for B 把A換成B**

May I exchange the blue T-shirt for a purple one?

我可以把藍色的T恤換成紫色的嗎？

2. **exchange for B 換成B**

This bank deals with exchange for foreign currencies.

這家銀行可處理外幣兌換。

主題 3

There be +名詞 + V-ing/p.p.　有…在做/被…

There are a lot of workers from this company going on a strike.
有很多該公司的員工走上街頭罷工。

There is a cat run over by a car on the highway.
高速公路上有一隻被車子輾過的貓。

延伸觀念：

名詞後面的which/who關係子句，可以省略關係代名詞who/which，後面的動詞改為分詞（主動語態改為V-ing；被動語態改為p.p.）

1. There are two boys playing in the playground.
   = There are two boys who are playing ....（主動語態）
   有兩個男生正在操場上玩遊戲。

2. There was a lot of trash littered on the ground.
   地上被丟滿了垃圾。
   = There was a lot of trash which was littered ....（被動語態）

換個對象寫寫看

Dear **Customer Service**,
I am writing to ask for an exchange for the pair of low rise jeans I recently purchased, Order Number 255121.

I like the color, cut, and the texture. Yet they don't fit me properly. The size 10 jeans are too loose on the waist and on the butt. That makes my bum look big on them!

I hope I can get a smaller size on return from your wonderful and well stocked store at your earliest convenience.

Sincerely,
Belle Tan

客服人員您好：
我寫信來要求將我買的低腰牛仔褲作換貨（訂單索引號碼**255121**）。

我喜歡它的顏色、剪裁、還有質感。但很遺憾的對我來說不合身。這件10號尺碼的牛仔褲在腰圍和臀部的部分都太鬆了。這讓我穿起來屁股看起來很大。
希望能盡速從你們款式齊全的店裡取得一件小尺碼的牛仔褲。

Belle譚 敬上

好用句型大補湯

商品描述和實際收到的不符

I'd like to exchange the backpack I purchased for a handbag of the same design. There is a large discrepancy between how the backpack is described and what I received. It was described as light-weight with lots of functional layers to hold a variety of items. But when I got it, I found it heavier than I expected and there are only three layers inside. I'd like to exchange for the handbag because it will be more useful to me.

我想要把我買的背包換成同款式的手提包。我拿到的背包和它當初的描述差很多。商品描述上寫說它重量很輕，有很多夾層可以擺放不同種類的東西。但實際拿到時我發現它比我預期來的重，且裡面只有三個夾層。我想要換同款手提包，因為比較實用。

因外觀和顏色而換貨

I'd like to exchange the pink skirt for the light-blue one of the same patterns. When I first saw the pink one on your TV shopping channel, the color seemed bright and rich. But when I received it, I am not very into the color because it's fading pink. Please send me the light-blue skirt.

我想把這件粉紅色裙子換成同花樣的淺藍色裙。當我在電視購物頻道上看到粉紅色裙時，我覺得它的色彩很亮很飽和。但當我拿到時，粉紅色看起來像褪色，我不是很喜歡。請換成淺藍色的。

其他要求換貨常見的萬用語：

1. The size 8 jeans don't fit well. They're good for my waist, but too tight through the thighs and butt. I'd like to exchange for a size 10.

   這件8號尺碼的牛仔褲不合身。雖然腰部剛好，但大腿到臀部的部分對我來說太緊。我想要換成10號尺碼。

2. I've found the size 23 shoes unfit. They are too tight for me. I'd like to exchange for size 24.

   我發現這雙23號的鞋子不合腳。他們太緊了。我想換成24號。

3. I don't like the texture of the leather boots. I'd like to exchange for suede of the same line.

   我不喜歡這雙皮製靴子的質感。我想換成同系列麂皮鞋。

主題 3

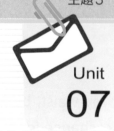

Unit
07
通知取貨

寫作策略

Step 1　**Who** are you writing to? 對象

Ms. Alice Lin

Step 2　**What** is this email for? 主旨

order-arrival for branch collection

Step 3　**Payment** status 付款狀態

already paid

Outline 這樣擬

商品已抵達　開場感謝對方購買某件商品，商品已抵達。

取貨細節　說明取貨及付款細節。

懇請回覆　要求對方回覆確認，希望對方儘早來取貨。

信　　尾　客套語＋署名。

Dear Ms. Lin,

We're pleased to inform you that the following items of your order No. 5212 have been dispatched to your chosen branch.

1 x wool Military Coat (size 10)
2 x washed T-shirt with pockets (beige, size 8)
1 x camouflage print trousers (size 8)

You are welcome to collect your order during our opening hours 11:00 a.m.～8:00 p.m. Tuesday through Sunday. You have paid the full amount of NT$ 8900 on June 23rd and there are no extra charges for the alteration to the length of the trousers.

Your continued patronage and suggestions are a vital part of our growth. And for that, we are the most grateful.
Thanks again! We look forward to serving you for many years to come.

Yours sincerely,
Susan Norms

主題 3

中文翻譯

林小姐您好：

您日前的訂單編號5212的商品已經送至您指定的門市了。商品明細如下：

1 x 羊毛海軍風外套 （尺碼8號）

2 x 水洗T恤（附口袋）（肉色，尺碼8號）

1 x 迷彩印花褲子 （尺碼8號）

歡迎您在門市營業時間（早上11點到晚上8點，週二到週日）到店取貨。您已經在6月23日付清所有款項，新台幣8900元。您訂購的褲子長度修改不另外收費。

您持續的光顧和給我們的建議一直是我們成長的重要動力，讓我們十分感激。

再次謝謝您。希望未來能為您服務長長久久。

Susan Norms敬上

關鍵單字片語

1. **dispatch**　*v.*　寄送 (= send)

We'll email you when your order is dispatched and also when it's ready to collect.

當您的訂購商品已經被寄出以及可以取貨時，我們會以電郵通知您。

2. **branch** *n.* 門市；分店；分公司
We have got the item you ordered from one of our branches.
我們已經從其中一家分店調貨取得您訂購的商品。

3. **collect** *v.* 取得；收集
Please feel free to collect your order at your nominated branch at your convenience.
歡迎在您有空時到您指定的門市取貨。

4. **opening hours** 營業時間
The opening hours of our campus branch are Monday - Friday: 09.00 - 18.00.
我們的學校門市部的營業時間是週一到週五早上九點到晚上六點。

5. **alteration** *n.* 修改
This tailor specializes in alterations, dressmaking, and tailoring, including wedding parties and prom dresses.
這位裁縫師專精服裝修改，訂製洋裝或量身訂做衣服，包含製作婚宴派對或畢業舞會用的洋裝。

6. **patronage** *n.* 光顧
Thank you for your past and continued patronage to our salon.
謝謝您過去和現在持續到我們美髮沙龍光顧。

給力句型解說 👆

過去分詞p.p.當形容詞

Thank you for your continued patronage.
謝謝您持續的光顧。

You can collect your ordered items at your chosen branch.
你可以在你指定的門市拿你訂的商品。

主題 **3**

延伸觀念：

1. **表示「被動」**

The stolen wallet was sent to Lost and Found.

被偷的錢包被送到失物招領處。

2. **表示「已經」**

The farmer picked up the fallen fruit, which was rotten to the core.

農夫撿起落果，都腐爛了。

3. **情緒動詞p.p.表示「感到」，形容人**

The farmer was very frustrated and depressed.

該名農夫覺得很沮喪和憂鬱。

for many years to come　在接下好幾年

We look forward to serving you for many years to come.

我們希望接下好幾年都可以繼續為您提供服務。

延伸句型：

n + to V 用「不定詞to V」修飾名詞：還有名詞要去做⋯

We still have a long way to go before there is an equal opportunity for all.

在人人機會真正平等之前，我們還有很長一段路要走。

He has nothing to do tonight.

他今晚沒事做。

He has few friends to play with.

他幾乎沒有朋友可以陪他玩。

換個對象寫寫看

Dear **Ms. Hsu**,

Thank you for placing an order at Mustbuy.com. **We are pleased to inform you the following items you ordered on June 24th (Order No. 5212) have arrived in the store**:

1 x High Rise Skinny Jeans (24 W)
2 x Boot Cut Jeans (23 W)
1 x Mid Rise Straight Fit Jeans (23 W)
1 x Low rise pipe jeans (24W)

You are welcome to collect your order during our opening hours Mon. -Sun.1:00 p.m.～10:00 p.m. The amount of the items is NT$12,900. We also charge alterations fee NT$500 for the low rise pipe jeans, so the total amount is NT$13,400. You have made part of a payment, NT$ 5,000 on June 22nd. Therefore, it leaves the debit payment NT$8,400 and please remit the payment when you collect the items.

Thanks again! We look forward to serving you soon.

Respectfully yours,
Cassie Chu

主題 3

許小姐您好：

謝謝您在Mustbuy.com上訂購產品。我們很高興通知您在6月24日下訂(編號5212)的商品已經抵達門市了。商品明細如下：

1 X 高腰顯瘦牛仔褲（24腰）

2 X小喇叭牛仔褲（23腰）

1 X中腰直筒緊身牛仔褲（23腰）

1 X低腰煙管褲（24腰）

歡迎您在門市營業時間（下午1點到晚上10點，週一到週日）到店取貨。商品金額小計12,900台幣。還要收取低腰煙管褲的修改費500元，總金額共134,000台幣。您已經在6月22日先付了新台幣5,000元。因此還有尾款8,400台幣，等取貨時付清。

再次謝謝您。希望能盡快為您服務。

Cassie 朱敬上

好用句型大補湯

只有付訂金，必須要付清尾款

You're welcome to visit the above retail branch to collect the goods. Please be notified that the total amount of the order is NT$8999. You have paid NT$2000. Please remit the debit payment of NT$6999 when you collect the items.

歡迎您到以上門市取貨。提醒您訂購品項的總金額是新台幣8999元。您已經先付了2000元，尚餘6999元，請在取貨時結清。

部分貨品已經沒有現貨或庫存

The washed T-shirts with pockets and camouflage print trousers you ordered have just arrived. As for the wool Military Coat (size 10), we're sorry it's out of stock due to high demand for this size. But we do have the same coat coming in other sizes for you choose from. If the other sizes don't fit, we'll return your prepaid amount NT$ 3999 for the coat.

您訂購的水洗T恤（附口袋）以及迷彩印花褲已經到貨了。至於羊毛軍裝風大衣（尺碼10號），因為這個尺碼很搶手，所以很抱歉已經沒有庫存。但我們有同款大衣的其他尺碼可供您挑選。若您試穿後覺得不合身，我們就會退還您預先付清該大衣的費用台幣3999元。

其他提醒取貨或沒有貨品的常用句型：

1. Thank you for considering our company. This email notification is to inform you that the order you placed last week has just hit the shelves. Please feel free to collect your merchandise at your convenience.

   謝謝您考慮本公司。這封信是要提醒您：您上週所下的訂單貨品已經抵達。歡迎您在有空時來取貨。

2. We are sorry to inform you that the office furniture set you requested last week is unavailable. However, we attached our latest office furniture catalog in case you want to consider other designs.

   我們很抱歉要通知您：您上週所訂購的辦公室家具目前沒有現貨。但我們附上最新一期家具目錄，也許您可以參考其他的款式。

主題 3

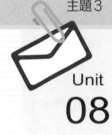

Unit
08　貨品瑕疵

寫作策略

Step 1 **Who** are you writing to? 你要寫給誰？

Mr. Johnson Lee

Step 2 **What** did the customer complain about? 客戶抱怨什麼？

defective goods

Step 3 **How** do you respond to the complaint? 你如何回應客訴？

apologies, compensation

Step 4 **What** will you deal with the problem?
你會如何處理這個問題？

refunds, exchange, not happening again

Outline 這樣擬

收到客戶反應　開場說明已收到顧客反映的問題，再陳述一次問題細節。

正在積極處理中　具體說明處理的方式和進度等細節。

懇請等候　懇請對方給你時間靜候處理結果。

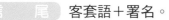

看看老師怎麼寫 🌐

Dear Mr. Lee,

We have received your email on June 23rd, claiming that you have found defects in the goods of our shipment. We were extremely sorry for the error, and we are dealing with the problem at this very moment.

We will certainly help with returns of the goods. We will send someone today to collect the entire shipment. In the meantime, we have already sent another shipment of perfect merchandise to you, which should arrive no later than tomorrow evening.

Please accept our sincere apologies for any inconvenience this may have caused. We assure you that we will take measures to maintain good quality to prevent any similar problems from happening again.

Sincerely yours,
Jack Middleson

主題 3

中文翻譯

李先生您好：

我們已收到您在6月23日的郵件，信中您提到在給您的貨物中貨品有出現瑕疵。我們對此失誤感到萬分抱歉，此刻正積極處理中。

我們當然會協助退貨。今天我們就會派人取回整批貨物。在此同時，我們也已經重新出貨，寄出完好無缺的貨品給您，應該明天傍晚前就會送達。

對任何可能造成您的不便，請接受我們誠摯的歉意。我們向您保證一定會採取措施維持好的品質，以確保類似問題不會再發生。

Jack Middleson 敬上

關鍵單字片語

1. **shipment**   *n.*   裝運；裝載的貨物

   The blockade prevented shipments of foreign food from reaching our shores.

   貿易封鎖使國外食品不能運抵我們的海岸。

2. **error**   *n.*   錯誤

   This error in transaction has caused him millions of dollars.

   交易過程的錯誤讓他損失好幾百萬美金。

3. **in the meantime**   同時 (= meanwhile)

   The police are tracking down the suspect. In the meantime, they have talked to all the witnesses.

警方正在追蹤這個嫌疑犯。在此同時，他們已經約談了所有證人。

4. **merchandise** *n.* 商品

This store is filled with merchandise exported from Korea.

這間店到處都是南韓進口的商品。

5. **assure** *v.* 向⋯保證

We assure you that we will take the responsibility and compensate your loss.

我們向您保證我們會負起責任並賠償您的損失。

6. **maintain** *v.* 維持 (= keep)

A good restaurant will maintain consistent good quality in both services and cuisine.

一間好的餐廳會維持服務和菜餚的一貫高品質。

給力句型解說

S + 助動詞 (can/should/may/must) + 原型動詞

This shipment you ordered should arrive no later than tomorrow evening.

您訂購的貨物應該會在明天傍晚前送達。

延伸觀念：

其他類似助動詞的用法

1. **ought to** + 原型動詞 = **should** + 原型動詞　應該

You ought to apologize to him. = You should apologize to him.

你應該向他道歉。

主題 3

2. **be able to** + 原型動詞 = **can** + 原型動詞 有能力會做

He is able to prepare dinner for 300 people.

= He can prepare dinner for 300 people.

他能為300人準備晚餐。

3. **have to** + 原型動詞 = **need to** + 原型動詞 = **must** + 原型動詞 必須去做

He has to/needs to finish the report tonight. = He must finish the report tonight.

他必須今晚完成報告。

S + 助動詞 (can/should/may/must) + have + p.p. 對過去事件的推測

1. **should + have + p.p.** 本來應該要做…（但結果沒做）

You should have told me the truth. Now I can't help you.

你早該跟我說實話的。現在我沒法幫你了。

2. **must + have p.p.** 一定已經…了（對過去事件十分有把握的肯定猜測）

The ground is wet. It must have rained earlier this afternoon.

地板是濕的。稍早一定下過雨。

3. **might/may + have p.p.** 應該已經…了（對過去事件沒有把握的猜測）

He hasn't come yet. He may have been caught in the traffic jam.

他還沒到。他現在可能塞在車陣裡。

4. **can't + have p.p.** 一定不可能已經…了（對過去事件很有把握的否定猜測）

He can't have gone to bed. The lights are still on in his room.

他不可能去睡了。他房間燈還亮著。

換個對象寫寫看

Dear **Ms. Chen**,
We were extremely sorry to know that you purchased 4 Maybelline Great Lash Mascara in your order No. 2512 but only received 2 in our shipment.

Please accept our sincere apologies for the errors in the shipment. We will deliver the rest of the items immediately, which will arrive no later than tomorrow afternoon. Besides, for compensation, we'll enclose a free sample for the latest BB cream in this shipment.

We hope you can forgive us for this unintentional mistake and continue to purchase goods from us.

Sincerely yours,
Jason Milton

陳小姐您好：
我們很抱歉得知在您的訂單號碼**2512**中，您原本訂購了**4**支**Maybelline Great Lash**睫毛膏，但實際收貨時只收到**2**支。

針對出貨過程的疏失，請接受我們誠摯的歉意。我們會立刻寄送短缺的貨品，貨物會在明天下午前送達。此外，為了彌補您，我們會附上一罐最新出的**BB**霜試用品。

我們希望您能原諒我們無意的疏失，並持續向我們訂購產品。

Jason Milton敬上

好用句型大補湯

交貨時間延遲

Please accept our apologies for the failure to deliver your ordered goods at the scheduled time in accordance with the contract we have signed. We were unable to fill all orders due to the excessive demand during the high season in the past two weeks. We have already sent the goods to you this morning. We'd like to inform you that we will still compensate you for your loss owing to the unintended violation of the contract terms.

我們很抱歉沒有按照合約上的預定時間寄出您訂購的貨品。因為前兩個禮拜旺季的需求太多，無法消化所有訂單。我們已經在今早送出貨品。我們要通知您因為意外違反合約，我們仍會賠償您的損失。

運送過程中貨品受損

We are extremely sorry to learn that your ordered goods were damaged on arrival. If we were to be responsible for the matter, we would replace these damaged items. However, as we confirmed with our warehouse staff, all the goods were carefully and perfectly packed and sent out in good condition. We have the clean B/L to prove this, and we have sent you a copy for your reference. It was evident that the damaged was caused due to careless handling in the shipping process. Please wait as we are currently negotiating with the shipping company as to how to settle the matter. We'll get back to you a.s.a.p.

我們很抱歉得知您所訂購的商品在抵達時受損。若我們要為此事負責,定當為您換貨。但我們和倉管人員確認過了,所有的貨物在出貨時,都是完好無缺,且都被仔細打包好才出貨。我們有提單可以證明,且也已經寄了一份副本給您參考。很明顯損害是在貨運過程中粗心所致。我們正在和貨運公司交涉如何處理此事,我們會儘快回覆給您。

其他回應顧客抱怨的萬用句型:

1. We are terribly sorry for damaging the goods you ordered.
   我們對於不小心毀損您的商品深感抱歉。

2. We will immediately send the rest of your ordered goods.
   我們會立刻寄送您訂單中短少的部分。

3. We sincerely apologize for the errors in shipment.
   我們為出貨過程的錯誤向您致歉。

4. We do apologize for damaging your goods during transportation.
   我們對於運送過程中造成商品的毀損感到抱歉。

主題 3

Unit 09　服務生態度差

寫作策略 🄰🄱

Step 1　**Who** are you writing to? 對象？

Holiday Inn

Step 2　**What** do you complain about? 抱怨什麼？

poor service/ incompetence and bad attitude of the personnel towards customer

Step 3　**Details** of the complaint 抱怨細節

problems

Step 4　**What** would you like the recipient to do?
你想要接待人員做什麼？

call to action: improve the quality of service/more training of the staff/ ask for proper apology from the personnel/company

Outline 這樣擬

寫信目的 開場可直接點名是來抱怨，或先說自己原本有很高期待，但卻得到令人失望的產品或服務。

問題核心 以陳述事實的口吻，點出服務不周處或產品的瑕疵。

敬請回覆 要求對方退換貨/退款，或純粹要求對方下次要改進。

信　　尾 客套語＋署名。

看看老師怎麼寫

To the Hotel Manager,

I am a frequent traveler and have been a loyal customer of your hotel for many years because I appreciate your emphasis on excellent service. But a recent episode at your hotel has made me question my loyalty.

I stayed in your hotel, room 203, from Monday, September 1st through Thursday, September 4th. Throughout my stay my towels were always dirty, and the bathroom plumbing was faulty. To make matters worse, one of my neighbors was very loud at night. I complained to the Front Desk Manager, Annie Shao, and requested another room but was told there were no other rooms available. Despite my repeated complaints, it was not until the third day of my stay that the plumbing was fixed and my towels changed. And no one from the hotel spoke to my noisy neighbor. Because of the noise, I was unable to sleep comfortably for two

主題 3

nights.

I hope this problem will be corrected prior to my next visit.
Thanks for your time and patience.

Sincerely,
Jenny Chen

中文翻譯

飯店經理您好：

我是個飛行常客，多年來是貴旅館的忠實顧客，因為我很欣賞你們強調高品質的服務。但最近一起事件讓我開始質疑我對你們的忠誠度。

我在9月1日（週一）到9月4日（週四）在貴旅館下榻四天。這段期間內，我的毛巾永遠都是髒的，而且浴室水管有問題。更糟的是，隔壁的房客晚上總是很吵。我有和櫃檯經理Annie Shao抱怨過，並要求換房。但我被告知沒有房間可換。且儘管我不斷反應，一直拖到下榻後三天，我的房間廁所才被修好，毛巾才換新。且飯店都沒有人幫我和隔壁的房客作溝通。因為噪音的關係，我有兩天晚上無法好好入睡。

我希望這個問題在我下次造訪前能有所改善。
謝謝您的時間和耐心。

Jenny 陳 敬上

關鍵單字片語

1. **loyal** *adj.* 忠實的

   Loyal customers keep coming back to the restaurant, for its outstanding services and good quality food.

   該餐廳因為有優越的服務品質和高水準的食物，讓忠實顧客不斷回籠。

2. **emphasis** *n.* 強調 (+ on ...)

   His English teacher puts emphasis on his reading proficiency.

   他的英文老師很注重他的閱讀能力。

3. **plumbing** *n.* 馬桶抽水

   We keep having problems with the plumbing.

   我們水管一直出問題。

4. **faulty** *adj.* （產品）有問題的

   Customers may ask for a refund if the goods are faulty.

   若產品有問題，顧客可能要求退費。

5. **complain** *v.* 抱怨 (+about某事；+ to 某人)

   The tenant complained to the landlord about the malfunction of the air-conditioner.

   這位房客向房東抱怨冷氣故障。

6. **to make things worse** 更糟的是

   The team has lost a series of games. To make things worse, its best pitcher got hurt yesterday.

   這球隊連輸了幾場比賽。更糟的是，隊上最好的投手昨天受傷了。

主題 3

給力句型解說 👉

despite + 名詞　儘管

1. **despite = in spite of = regardless of**：後面接「名詞」
   He went to school despite/in spite of/regardless of the heavy rain.
   儘管/雖然下大雨，他還是去上學。

2. **although = despite the fact that**：後面接「子句」
   He went to school although/despite the fact that it rained heavily.
   儘管/雖然下大雨，他還是去上學。

it is/was not until ... that ...　直到…才…

It is not until one gets sick that he understands the importance of health.

= One doesn't understand the importance of health until he gets sick.

直到生病了，人才會了解健康的重要性。

延伸觀念：

強調句句型It is/was ...that ...，將原本句子裡要強調的部分放在is/was後面。

The customer complained about the leak to the hotel manager at midnight.

1. **強調主詞the customer:** It was the customer that complained about the leak...

2. **強調受詞about the leak:** It was about the leak that the customer complained to the manager ...

3. 強調受詞to the manager: It was to the manager that the customer complained about the leak …
4. 強調時間副詞at midnight: It was at midnight that the customer complained to the manager …

換個對象寫寫看

To **the Heart Restaurant**,

Up until recently we have enjoyed coming to the Heart for the food and the service. Unfortunately, after our visit last Friday, has made us change our perception .

Last Friday we took our family and friends to the restaurant. Instead of the usual delightful service, we encountered problems almost at every turn. The issue started when our reservation for eight was pushed back because of overfilled capacity and we were forced to wait for more than 30 minutes. We were finally given a round table which was crowded for a group of eight. The next problem occurred when half of the order was mixed up and had to be returned.

Our experience was not near what we had come to expect from the Heart. Hopefully, you will be able to return to your previous level of excellence.

Sincerely,

主題 3

Harvey Harman

飯店經理您好：
一直到最近我們都很喜歡到貴餐廳用餐享受美食和服務。但不幸的是，我們上週五用餐的經驗讓我們對於你們的想法有了改觀。

上週五我們帶家人和朋友到貴餐廳。不同於以往的優質服務，我們幾乎每一個環節都遇到問題。首先是因為客滿的關係，我們八人的訂位被延後了，我們被迫多等**30**分鐘。等我們終於有一張桌子後，發現桌子對八個人來說實在太擠。接下來的問題是我們點的餐點將近一半被弄錯了，必須退回。

我們此行的經驗和我們原本預期得到的不成正比。希望你們能恢復之前高品質的服務水準

Harvey Harmna　敬上

好用句型大補湯

服務人員訓練或專業度不足

I'm writing to complain that your hotel staff portrayed a large amount of incompetence and lack of professionalism during my stay from the 1st of September to the 4th. After the bellman took my baggage to my room, I found the edges of one baggage slightly damaged for being dragged along on the floor. Besides, the cleaning staff often forgot to change my towels and they even forgot to lock the door when they left.

我寫信來抱怨在我9月1日到4日下榻貴旅館期間，你們旅館人員不斷呈現他們的無能和缺乏專業。當門房幫我把行李搬到房間時，我發現其中一個行李箱邊緣有輕微損傷，應該是因為在地板上拖行造成的。此外，清潔人員常忘了替換毛巾，甚至離開房間時忘了鎖門。

其他抱怨信常見的萬用語：

1. My major/main complaint is about the poor service I received during my stay at your hotel.
   我主要的抱怨是在貴旅館下榻時，我得到的服務品質極差。

2. I'm not content with/satisfied with/happy with/very frustrated about/disappointed about the poor services provided during my stay.
   我很不高興/不滿意/不開心/很灰心/很失望在我下榻期間，你們所提供的服務品質很差。

3. I am writing to encourage you to improve your customer service.
   我寫信希望鼓勵你們要改善你們的客服品質。

4. I hope you pay more attention to the improvement of your service, and take an immediate action to solve the problems.
   我希望你們要注意改善你們的服務，並立即採取行動解決問題。

主題 3

主題4　愛旅遊，玩社交！

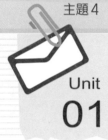

Unit
01
套裝行程

寫作策略 ⒶⒷ

Step **1** **Who** are you writing to? 這封感謝函是要給誰？

Easy Vacation

Step **2** **What** can the travel agency help you with?
旅行社能協助什麼？

booking

Step **3** **Details** of your request/trip 特殊要求 / 旅行的細節

destination, dates, requirements, numbers of rooms,
special needs

Outline 這樣擬

主要需求 開場告知旅程的目的地，以及出發和回程時間。

細　　節 詳述對旅館、機票的需求細節。

敬請回覆 請對方提供相關旅遊資訊供你選擇。

信　　尾 客套語＋署名。

看看老師怎麼寫

To **Whom It May Concern**,

My husband and I are interested in your special summer offers. We would like you to help book **flights** and hotels for our family trip to Tokyo. We plan to **depart** from Kaohsiung on Aug 8th and return on Aug 13th.

Regarding the **return tickets**, we prefer China **Airlines**. **As for** accommodation, we'd like to stay at a five star hotel with easy access to the **metro**. **Since** we'll bring our five-year-old son and my two parents with us, we need to book two rooms, one suite and one double.

Thank you for your prompt attention to the above and I look forward to receiving your email.

Kind regards,
Jasmine Lu

主題 4

敬啟者：

我先生和我對您們的夏日優惠方案很感興趣。我們想請您幫忙訂購我們到東京家族旅行的機加酒行程。我們計畫八月八日從高雄出發，八月十三日回台。

我們偏好向華航訂來回機票。關於住宿的部分，我們希望住在距離捷運站近的五星級旅館。因為我們會帶五歲的兒子和我的父母一同出遊，所以我們需要兩個房間，一間套房和一間雙人房。

謝謝您迅速為我們處理以上事宜，期待您的email回覆。

Jasmine 盧　敬上

關鍵單字片語

1. **To Whom It May Concern** 敬啟者（信件開頭稱謂語）
2. **flight** *n.* 班機
   Ben caught the first flight out of Washington this morning for Tokyo.
   Ben搭乘今早最早一班離開華盛頓的班機前往日本。
3. **depart** *v.* 離開；出境
   Dan departed from Taipei for Shanghai last Friday on business.
   Dan上週五搭機從台北去上海出差。
   departure *n.*
   depart from 從……離開；depart for 前往……

4. **return ticket** 來回票

Make sure you book return tickets instead of one-way tickets on the website.

要確定你在網路上訂的是來回票而不是單程票。

one-way ticket 單程票

5. **airlines** *n.* 航空公司

China airlines have been providing direct flights across the Straits in the past three years.

華航過去這三年來提供兩岸直航的服務。

6. **metro** *n.* 捷運、地鐵

This hotel is within walking distance to the nearest metro station.

這家旅館步行即可抵達距離最近的捷運站。

給力句型解說

> **as for / regarding + 名詞 至於、關於…**

Regarding/As for your application, we'll proceed it as soon as possible.

關於你的申請案，我們會盡速處理。

延伸觀念：

concerning

with regard to + N. 關於……

Relating to

about

I'm calling concerning/with regard to/regarding/about/as for my application to the position.
我來電了解我求職應徵的事。

since　既然……

Since you have nothing to do tomorrow, why don't we see a movie together?
既然你明天沒事，我們何不一起去看電影？

比較**since**的用法：

1. **自從……**

   I haven't heard anything from you since I moved to Japan.
   自從我搬到日本後，就沒聽到你的消息了。

2. **既然……** (= as, because)

   Since I will be back to Taiwan in two days, we can meet and catch up then.
   既然我再過兩天會回台灣，我們到時可以見面敘舊。

換個對象寫寫看

To Whom It May Concern,
My wife and I would like you to help book flights and hotels for our family trip to Seoul. We plan to depart from Taipei on Dec 5th and return on Dec 9th.

Since we're heading for the most popular ski resort, The Ski

Paradise, **we'd like to book a room for 2 adults and 2 children directly inside the resort villa for four nights. We also need you to sign up the local ski courses for my two kids.**

Please forward me the details of the flight and hotel packages. Thank you for your prompt attention to the above and I look forward to hearing from you soon.

Regards,
Julie Fan

敬啟者：
我太太和我想請您幫我們全家韓國首爾之行訂購機加酒行程。我們計畫**12月5日**從台北出發，**12月9日**回台。
因為我們要去當地最熱門的滑雪聖地──滑雪天堂，我們想要直接在滑雪度假村內訂一房（兩大兩小）過四個晚上。我們也要請您協助幫兩個孩子報名滑雪課程。
請提供機票和訂房資料。

謝謝您迅速為我們處理以上事宜，期待您的回覆。

Julie 范　敬上

主題4

好用句型大補湯

對飯店地點軟、硬體設施的需求

We'd like to stay at a centrally-located hotel which is located near major attractions, or at least with easy access to public transportations. We prefer hotels that run shuttles to and from popular sightseeing destinations, or are possible to get to places on foot. Besides, my parents are both over 75 and disabled, so we are looking for hotels which are wheelchair accessible with widened doorways. It's best to have internet connection, sauna, and Jacuzzi, in the rooms.

我們想要找位於樞紐地帶，且鄰近主要娛樂景點的旅館，至少要能很快就通達大眾交通工具。我們偏愛提供接駁車來往熱門觀光景點，或可以步行抵達景點的旅館。此外，我的父母年紀都超過75歲且身體不便，所以我們在找輪椅可以通行且門前走道較寬敞的旅館。最好房間提供上網、蒸汽浴和按摩浴缸等設施。

對機票的需求

We are looking for the cheapest flight deals. Direct flights are desirable, but long stopovers or transit flights are not a problem.

我們在找票價最便宜的機票。直達票當然最好，但我們也可以接受中途需過境等候較久或需轉機的機票。

其他詢問旅遊資訊的萬用語：

1. Would you please send us a list of suggested hotels with prices?
   你能寄給我們您所推薦的旅館清單，並附上住房價格嗎？

2. We would very much appreciate if you can send us recommended tour packages and detailed itinerary.
   若您可以提供您所推薦的旅遊行程和詳細行程表，我們將不勝感激。

3. We will be glad to receive your suggested hotel and flight packages.
   若能收到你推薦的機加酒行程，我們會很高興。

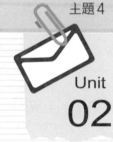

Unit 02 簽證申請

寫作策略 AB

Step 1　**Who** are you writing to? 寫給誰？

Mr. Wills

Step 2　**What type** of visa are you applying for?

申請什麼樣的簽證？

tourist visa

Step 3　**Details** of visa application 簽證申請書的細節

application, progress

Outline 這樣擬

目　　的	開場直接說明你要詢問簽證的近況。
細　　節	告知簽證申請時間和細節。
敬請回覆	請對方回覆。
信　　尾	客套語＋署名。

Dear Mr. Wills,

I'm writing this letter to ask about the **status** of my tourist visa application to Korea, which **was lodged** on Dec 15th. My application **reference** number is Z00325.

I learned from your website that visa **processing** time is approximately 7 to 10 working days. It's been two weeks since I submitted my application, and I'd like to know **whether** my visa **has been issued**, or when it **will be granted**.

Please help me check my visa application **progress** and let me know if I need to provide any further documents.
Hope to hear from you soon.

Regards,
Benson Chu

中文翻譯

親愛的Wills先生：

我寫這封信是為了詢問我的韓國旅遊簽證申請進度。我是在12月15日提出申請，申請索引號碼是Z00325。

我從你們網路上得知簽證處理時間約在7到10個工作天。從我申請到現在已經兩個禮拜了，我想知道簽證是否已經核發，或何時會被核發。

請幫我查詢簽證申請現況，讓我知道我是否需要補繳文件。
希望盡速得到您的回覆。

Benson Chu 敬上

關鍵單字片語

1. **status**　*n.*　狀態 (= condition, position, situation)
   What's your marital status? Are you married or not?
   你的婚姻狀態為何？已婚或未婚？

2. **lodge**　*v.*　提出　(= submit, hand in)
   He lodged an appeal with the High Court.
   他向高等法院提出上訴。

3. **reference**　*n.*　參考
   These students checked out a lot of reference books for their research.
   這些學生借閱了很多參考書，以協助他們做研究。

4. **process**　*v.*　處理

Are you experienced in using the updated word-processing software?

你很熟悉如何操作這個更新版文書處理軟體嗎？

5. **issue**　*v.*　核發 (= grant, approve of)

The US State department issues millions of passports each year.

美國政府每年核發數百萬的護照。

6. **progress**　*n.*　進度

Please keep me posted of the progress of the event.

請隨時告知我這起事件的最新發展。

主題 4

給力句型解說 👉

be + p.p. 被動語態

	主動語態	被動語態
現在簡單式	He waters the flowers every day.	The flowers are watered every day.
過去簡單式	He watered the flowers yesterday.	The flowers were watered yesterday.
現在進行式	He is watering the flowers now.	The flowers are being watered now.
未來簡單式	He will water the flowers tomorrow.	The flowers will be watered tomorrow.
現在完成式	He has watered the flowers already.	The flowers have been watered already.
結合助動詞	He may water the flowers later.	The flowers may be watered later.

whether / if + S + V　間接問句：是否……

注意：Yes /No問句改成間接問句時，主詞在動詞之前，動詞注意時態變化。

Does he **live** in Taipei? → Can you tell me if/whether he **lives** in Taipei.

Did he **call** you last night? → I wonder if/whether he **called** you last night.

Have they **arrived** yet? → I don't know if/whether they **have arrived** yet.

Is he **ready** now? → Let me know if/whether he **is ready** now.

比較：**whether / if** 不同處： **whether**可和**or not**連用；但**if**不能和**or not** 連用。

Tell me **whether/if** he will come to my party.
= Tell me **whether** he will come **or not**.
告訴我他是否會來我的派對。

換個對象寫寫看

To **Whom It May Concern**,
I'm writing this letter to ask about the status of my working visa application to China, which was lodged on Nov. 10th. My application reference number is CT0352.
It's been two weeks since I submitted my application, **I was wondering if it was still being processed. Can you kindly inform me when my visa will be issued?**

Thank you for your prompt attention, and I look forward to hearing from you soon.

Sincerely,
Kelly Hsiao

主題 4

敬啟者:

我寫這封信是為了詢問我的大陸工作簽證申請進度。我是在**11月10日**提出申請,申請索引號碼是**CT0352**。

從我申請到現在已經兩個禮拜了,我想知道簽證申請案是否仍在處理中。可否請您告訴我簽證何時會核發?

感謝您迅速處理我的詢問,期待能盡速收到您的消息。

Kelly 蕭 敬上

好用句型大補湯

詢問學生簽證延長效期進度

Can you please help me check the status of my student visa application to the U.K.? My visa application reference number is _____. On _____ I applied to extend my current student visa for another six months, in order to complete my postgraduate programs in London.

您能否幫我檢查我的英國學生簽證申請現況?我的簽證申請索引代號是……。我在_____月_____日提出簽證延長效期,希望延長6個月效期,以在倫敦完成我的碩士學位。

詢問打工度假簽證進度

I will highly appreciate if you can check the progress of my Australia working holiday visa? My TRN (transaction reference number) is _____. My application was lodged online on Dec.

15th, and I have complete health check and submitted the financial statement. Please inform me of the latest status.

若您能協助檢查我的澳洲打工度假簽證申請進度，我將萬分感激。我的交易索引號碼是……。我在12月15日上網完成線上申請，且已經完成健康檢查並繳交財力證明文件。請通知我最新的進度。

其他請求協助確認資訊的句型：

1. I will be very grateful if you can inform me of the progress of my visa application.

   若您能告知我的簽證申請進度，我將十分感謝。

2. Can you kindly help confirm if my visa has been issued?

   能否請您確認我的簽證是否已經核發下來了？

3. Would you please notify me of the progress of my visa application? Your efforts will be highly appreciated.

   您能否通知我簽證申請進度？您的協助，我將感激不盡。

主題 4

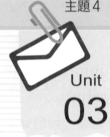

Unit
03
旅客登機資訊

寫作策略 🅰🅱

Step 1 **Who** will receive this letter? 誰會收到這封信？

Ms. Ma, travel agent

Step 2 **What** is the purpose of the letter? 這封信的主旨

inform details of reservation

Step 3 **Details** listed on the boarding pass 登機證上的細節

name of the passenger, origin, destination, flight number, boarding gate, boarding hour, class, date, time

Step 4 **Other Rules** 其他規定

free, 2 pieces, 20kg

Outline 這樣擬 ✏️

破　　題　開場直接說明以下提供旅客的登機資料。

旅客登機資料　詳述登機時間、班機資訊。

注意事項　提醒登機須注意事項。

信　尾　客套語＋署名。

看看老師怎麼寫

Dear Ms. Chou,

I'm very pleased to inform you we've completed the flight reservation for Ms. Chen Mei-Ru. **The following are** the details of your reservation.

Name of the passenger: Ms Chen Mei-Ru
Origin: Taipei, Taiwan (R.O.C)
Destination: New York, the U.S.A.
Flight Number: B3120
Boarding Gate: Gate 21
Boarding time: 07:30 a.m.
Seat: Z07 (**Aisle**)
Class: **economic**
Date and Time of departure: 08:15 am, Sept 9th, 2015

The flight **itinerary** will be sent to your email address. Please forward to your client and confirm **the above** information.
Please also inform Ms. Chen of the following rules.
1. Please arrive at the airport at least 90 minutes **prior to** the boarding time.
2. Each passenger is permitted one piece of **carry-on luggage**.
3. Free baggage **allowance**:

(1) Piece：2 pieces

(2) Weight：Each piece must not weigh more than 20 kg.

Thank you very much.

Sincerely,

Jenny Lai

中文翻譯

親愛的周小姐：

我們很開心通知您：您幫陳美如小姐預定的機票已經訂好了。以下是登機資料：

旅客姓名：陳美如

出發地：台灣台北

目的地：美國紐約

班機號碼：B3120

登機門：21號門

登機時間：上午7點半

座位號碼：Z07（靠走道）

艙等：經濟艙

出發日期與時間：2015年9月9日，上午8點15分

班機行程表會寄發到您的電子信箱。請與客戶確認以上資料正確。

也請轉達陳小姐以下登機規定：

1. 請在登機時間前90分鐘抵達機場。

2. 每位旅客只能攜帶一件機上行李。

3. 免費托運行李：兩件，個別重量在20公斤以下。

非常感謝您。

Jenny 賴　敬上

關鍵單字片語

1. **boarding gate** 登機門

   Passengers to Flight No. T312, please go to Boarding Gate No.12.

   搭乘T312班機的旅客，請前往12號登機門。

2. **aisle** *n.*　走道

   Most travelers prefer window seats to aisle seats for the view.

   大部分的旅客，因為視野的關係，偏愛靠窗的座位勝過靠走道的座位。

3. **economic** *n.*　經濟艙

   A free airline upgrade to business class or first class is the holy grail for many travellers.

   對很多旅客來說，從經濟艙免費升等到商務艙是他們心中的聖盃。

4. **itinerary** *n.*　路線 (= schedule, timetable)

   Please leave me a copy of your itinerary in case of emergency.

   請讓我保留一份你的旅遊行程表，以防萬一。

5. **carry-on luggage** *n.*　機上行李

   Each passenger is allowed to take one piece of carry-on luggage of less than 10 kg.

主題4

每位乘客可以攜帶一件10公斤內的機上行李。

6. **allowance**　*n.*　允許

Sales staff get a generous mileage allowance or a company car.

公司業務員可使用很大額度的公司車里程數。

給力句型解說 👉

> **the following** 以上的，上述的
> **the above** 以下的，下列的
> **the following/the above**後面的動詞，以後方名詞的單複數決定動詞單複數。

The following/above are the tips for this middle-age woman to stay young.

以下/以上是這位中年美魔女維持年輕的秘訣。

The following are the tips to make your ends meet.

以下是維持收支平衡的一些秘訣。

The above is his explanation to the economic downturn.

以上是他對經濟衰退原因的解釋。

> **prior to + N.**　在…之前

Please make the payment at least 3 days prior to the departure time.

請在啟程日前3天完成付費。

延伸觀念：

「在…之前」相關片語

1. **in advance / before hand：放在動詞之後或句尾**

   You need to file your leaving request one week in advance.

   你必須在一週前提出請假申請。

2. **before：連接兩個句子作為連接詞**

   You need to file the request one week before you take the day off.

   你要在休假一週前提出申請。

MEMO

Dear Ms. Wang,

Thank you very much for booking a flight with Best Airlines. We've completed your flight reservation. The details are as follows. Since you are an honored member of Best airline, We're very pleased to inform you that you have been upgraded to fly in business class for your trip to Hong Kong.

Name of the passenger: Ms. Cindy Wang
Origin: Taipei, Taiwan (R.O.C)
Destination: Hong Kong, China
Flight Number: B580
Boarding Gate: Gate 8
Boarding Hour: 16:30
Seat: Z07
Class: business
Date and Time of departure: 17:15, Dec. 31, 2015

The flight itinerary will be sent to your email address. Please confirm the above information.

Thank you again for flying with us, and we look forward to serving you soon.

Regards,
Mandy Chou

親愛的王小姐：

謝謝你選擇向倍斯特航空訂位。我們已為您訂好機位了。以下是訂位資料。
由於您是我們尊榮的常客，很開心通知您我們已為您免費升等，讓您乘坐商
務艙去香港。

旅客姓名：Cindy Wang

出發地：台灣台北

目的地：香港

班機號碼：**B580**

登機門：**8**號門

登機時間：下午**4**點半

座位號碼：**Z07**

艙等：商務艙

出發日期與時間：**2015**年**12**月**31**日，**17**點**15**分

班機行程表會寄發到您的電子信箱。請確認以上資料正確。

再次感謝您選擇搭乘倍斯特航空，期待很快再為您服務。

Mandy 周　敬上

好用句型大補湯 📋

更改訂位紀錄

With reference to your previous email requesting changing the departure time/date, we'd like to inform you the reservation has been amended to your needs. Here are the details. Please also be aware that we charge $50 change fee.

關於您上次來信提到要更改班機啟程日期與時間，要通知您我們已經依照您的需求更改訂位紀錄了。以下是登機細節。請注意我們會收取50美金的訂位更改手續費。

信用卡付費確認訂位

To complete the flight reservation, please offer the following payment information.

・Credit card type
・Credit card number/expiration date and card verification number
・Card holder's full name and billing address

為了確認訂位，請提供以下付款資訊：

・信用卡卡別
・信用卡號碼／失效日期／卡片背面末三碼
・持卡人全名與帳單寄送地址

請對方「確認」資料的萬用句型：

1. Can you review the attached boarding details and reply with confirmation?

   可否請您過目附件的登機資料細節並回信確認？

2. We'd be much grateful if you can confirm the following/above flight reservation details within 12 hours upon receiving this mail.

   若您能在收到此信12小時內確認以下／以上的班機訂位資訊，我們將十分感激。

3. Please kindly check the enclosed flight reservation details and confirm if the information is correct at your earliest convenience.

   請查閱附件的班機訂位資訊，並請盡速撥冗確認資料是否正確無誤。

主題4

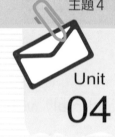

Unit 04　預訂房間

寫作策略 AB

Step 1　**Who** are you writing to? 對象

the hotel manager

Step 2　The information of making a room **reservation** 訂房資訊

guest name, arrival date, departure date, number of rooms, accommodations, rate per night

Step 3　Detailed **requests / requirements** of your stay

詳細的住房需求

room amenities, facilities & services

Outline 這樣擬

訂房需求　開場直接說明你要訂房，簡述房間數量，下榻日期。

需求細節　告知對方所需提供的服務。

敬請回覆　請對方回覆。

信　　尾　客套語＋署名。

看看老師怎麼寫

Dear Sir/Ma'am,

Our company has decided to stay at your hotel for our incentive tour on December 20th, 2015, for a duration of 3 days. We plan to book 30 rooms to accommodate an approximate number of 80 people.

Prior to our confirmation, we would like to know about tourist group packages. Please send me the list of room types and current group rates.

Our requests for accommodation are as follows. We prefer well-furnished suites, with separate bath and toilet, and wireless internet in each room. We also want rooms on lower level floor. And can you get us rooms next to each other?

I would appreciate it if you can reply to the above inquiries by tomorrow.

Regards,
Frank Chian
the HR manager of IBM Corporation

中文翻譯

親愛的先生/女士：

我們公司已決定今年員工旅遊要在貴酒店住房，從2015年12月20日起下榻3天。我們計畫訂30間房，以容納大約80人。

在我們確認下訂前，我們想知道團體旅客住房方案。請給我們房型列表和現在的團體住房房價。

以下是我們的住房要求。我們希望訂裝潢舒適的套房，淋浴間和廁所隔開，每間房都要能無線上網。我們也想要低樓層的房間，此外可否請您讓我們的房間集中彼此相鄰？

若您能在明天前回覆以上詢問，我將十分感激。

Frank 簡 敬上

關鍵單字片語

1. **incentive tour** 員工旅遊

   The employees get to vote for the destination and package for their annual incentive tour.

   這些員工可以投票決定年度員工旅遊的目的地以及行程。

   incentive *adj.* 激勵的

2. **duration** *n.* 期間

   The course of Hotel Management is of three-month duration.

   這一門旅館管理的課程為期三個月。

3. **current** *adj.* 現在的 (= present)

In its current state, the car is worth NT$10,000.

以這部車現在的車況來看，它價值十萬元。

4. **well-furnished** *adj.* 裝潢很好的

We enjoyed a pleasant weekend at the well-furnished family room.

我們在這裝潢良好的家族套房度過很棒的週末。

5. **separate** *adj.* 分開的，分別的 (=divided)

The kids stay in the separate room, each with a computer.

孩子們待在不同的房間，每間都有自己的電腦。

6. **wireless** *adj.* 無線的

The city government provides free wireless access to the Internet in public areas.

市政府在公共地區提供無線上網服務。

給力句型解說

a number of + 複數可數名詞　數量為…

an amount of + 不可數名詞

The science team is working on a large number of experiments.

這個科學團隊正在進行為數眾多的實驗。

USB technology benefits a huge number of gadgets.

隨插隨使用的科技造福大量的電子產品。

A large amount of money was stolen from the bank.

大量的金錢從這家銀行被竊取。

主題 4

...is/are as follows　……如下

The winners are as follows: Mandy, Sandy, and Hannah.
= The following are the winners, Mandy, Sandy, and Hannah.
優勝者如下：Mandy, Sandy還有Hannah。

注意：**as follows/the following** 搭配的 **be**動詞依據提及的名詞單複數作變化。
The reasons why I am against smoking are as follows.
我反對抽煙的理由如下。
The result of the competition is as follows.
比賽結果如下。

換個對象寫寫看

Dear **Sir/Ma'am**,
I'm arranging a trip for my two Japanese clients, Mr. Ichiro Takashi and Mr. Davishi Kenji. I'd like to book a deluxe twin room for them to stay at your hotel from Feb 5th to 7th.

Their requests for accommodation are as follows. They hope the room can be equipped with a/c, broadband Internet access, coffee and tea making facilities, and an LCD TV with Satellite Channels. They also request for taxis to shopping and sightseeing destinations. They also like to have an interpreter for their day tour on Feb 6th.

Can you reply to me if you can meet the above requests as soon as possible?

Hope to hear from you soon.

Regards,
Belle Hsieh

親愛的先生／女士：

我正在幫我的兩個日本客戶Ichiro Takashi 和Davishi Kenji先生安排旅遊行程。我想要訂一間兩單人床的房間，讓他們在2月5日到7日期間在你們旅館下榻。

以下是他們的住房要求。他們希望房間有空調、寬頻上網、咖啡或茶水沖泡設備，以及可收看衛星頻道的液晶電視。
他們也要求你們可以提供接駁車載他們去購物或觀光景點，也希望2月6日的旅遊能有口譯人員陪同。

您能盡速回覆是否能滿足以上需求嗎？

期待盡快得到您的回覆。

Belle 謝 敬上

好用句型大補湯

房間內部設備

I'd like to book a deluxe suite with an ocean view. I hope it can also be equipped with high-speed Internet access, flat screen color television and home theater. Please also provide an iron and ironing board. I also want a Jacuzzi in the bathing area.

我想要有海景的豪華套房，我希望房間可以高速上網，配備有平板彩色電視和家庭劇院組。也請提供熨斗和燙衣板。我也想要浴室裡有按摩浴缸。

飯店設施與服務

Since I'm traveling with my wife and two children under the age of five, I'd like to request for babysitting and child-care services during the day while we're out for sightseeing. I'd like to make an appointment with your spa salon for my wife, so she can enjoy the manicure, pedicure, facial and whole-body massage services.

因為我和我太太以及兩個5歲以下孩童一起出遊，我們想要白天出外觀光時，請你們協助看護孩童。我也要幫我太太向你們的水療沙龍預約，這樣她可以享受你們的美甲、作臉以及全身按摩等服務。

其他訂房要求的萬用句型：

1. A small but decently furnished and well-ventilated room would be quite enough for me.
   一個小但裝潢精美且通風良好的房間對我來說就足夠了。

2. I would prefer an accommodation on the ground floor.
   我偏好一樓的房間。

3. Please confirm reservation for one double bed / single bed room with air-conditioning.
   請幫我確認預訂一個雙人床／單人床房間，附有空調冷氣。

主題 4

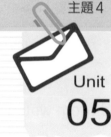

Unit
05

加床服務

寫作策略 A B

Step **1** **Who** are you writing to? 對象

hotel manager

Step **2** Make a room **reservation** 預訂房間

guest name, arrival date, departure date, number of rooms, accommodations, rate per night

Step **3** **Request** for extra-beds/cots/cribs and/or children 需求

Outline 這樣擬

訂房需求 開場直接說明你要訂房，簡述房間數量，下榻日期。

提出加床需求 詢問對方可否加床以及是否額外收費。

敬請回覆 請對方回覆。

信 尾 客套語＋署名。

看看老師怎麼寫

Dear Sir / Ma'am,

My wife and I plan to book our stay at your hotel for our family trip to Hualian. We'd like to check in on June 21st and check out on the 23rd (2 nights). Please reserve a standard double room for our stay-over.

Considering our 7-year-old daughter will be staying with us, too. we would like to know about your policies for children sharing the room with parents. Do you accept our request for an extra bed? If it's OK, how much do you charge for add-on beds?

Your early reply to the above matters will be highly appreciated.

Warm regards,
Peter Jennings

主題 4

中文翻譯

親愛的先生／女士：

我太太和我打算家族旅遊花蓮時在貴旅館住2晚。我們打算在6月21日下榻，23日離開（兩晚）。請幫我們訂一間標準雙人房。

考慮到我們7歲的女兒也會同行，我們想知道你們針對兒童和父母同住一間的收費規定。你們可否接受我們要求加一張床？如果可以的話，加張床的額外收費為何？

若您能盡速回覆以上事項，我們將不勝感激。

Peter Jennings敬上

關鍵單字片語

1. **check in** 住房登記

   Most hotels allow customers to check in after 3:00 pm.

   大部分飯店讓顧客下午三點以後辦住房登記。

2. **check out** 退房手續

   Customers need to complete check-out procedures by 12:00 p.m.

   顧客要在中午12點前辦妥退房手續。

3. **policy** *n.* 法規 (= regulation, rule)

   Cancellation and prepayment policies vary according to the room type.

   訂房取消或預繳訂金的規定依訂房房型不同而有所差別。

4. **accept**　*v.*　接受

Only a few hotels can accept last-minute cancellation of reservation.

只有少數旅館可以接受最後一刻取消訂房。

5. **extra**　*adj.*　額外的

Any type of extra bed or cot is upon request and needs to be confirmed by the hotel.

任何形式的追加床組或搖床都必須先提出申請，且要經過飯店同意。

6. **charge**　*v.*　收費（也可當名詞）

One child over 12 years old or adult is charged NT$ 800 per night and person in an extra bed.

12歲以上兒童或成人，每加一床每晚要多付800元。

主題 4

給力句型解說 👆

介系詞「for + 名詞」常見涵義

1. **為了…；因為 表「目的、原因」**

   Please reserve a standard double room for our stay-over.

   請幫我們訂一間過夜的標準雙人房。

2. **對於…關於 表「主題，對象」**

   I'd like to know about your hotel policies for children.

   我想要了解關於兒童住房的規定。

3. **達，計 表「時間、距離」**

   He has been watching TV for an hour.

   他已經看了一個小時的電視。

4. **當作 表「代表、作為」**

   We use boxes for chairs.

   我們用紙箱當椅子。

5. **贊成 表「支持」**

   More than 30% of the citizens are for death penalty.

   超過3成的公民贊同死刑。

6. **朝向 表「方向」**

   He left/headed for Taipei last night.

   他昨晚前往台北。

介系詞「to + 名詞」常見涵義

1. **往、到、向　表「方向」**

   He took a trip to Taipei with his friends.

   他和朋友去台北旅遊。

2. **（變）成，（變）到　表「轉變、趨勢」**

   Things went from bad to worse.

   情勢越來越糟。

3. **直到，達　表「時間、程度、範圍」**

   He worked from day to midnight.

   他從早工作到午夜。

4. **對、向　表「對象」**

   He handed in his resignation letter to his supervisor.

   他遞交辭呈給長官。

5. **屬於　表「歸屬」**

   I bought a ticket to the concert, but lost my key to the door.

   我買了演唱會門票，卻把家門鑰匙搞丟。

主題 4

換個對象寫寫看

To **the Hotel Manager**,

Two of my friends and I are planning to stay at your hotel for one night on Saturday, May 5th. Please kindly book a deluxe twins room for our stay-over. Since there are three of us sharing one room, we would like to know about your policies for extra beds. **Is it OK to book one extra bed in our twins room? If that's fine, can you tell us how will you charge the extra bed?**

Thank you and we look forward to your earliest reply.

Sincerely,
Sandy Summers

飯店經理您好：

我和我兩個朋友計畫要在**5月5**日週六在你們旅館下榻一晚。煩請幫我們訂一間豪華雙人房（兩張單人床）。因為我們三個人要同住一間房，想要知道你們對於加床的收費規定。我們可以在雙人房裡加一張床嗎？如果可以的話，能否請您告知如何收費？

感謝您，也期待您能盡快回覆。

Sandy Summers 敬上

好用句型大補湯

確認加床不加價的服務是否屬實

I've checked your hotel policies from your website. It says children are allowed to stay in the room with parents either with or without an extra bed with NO EXTRA charge if they are under twelve years of age. I'd like to confirm if my acknowledgement to the above policies is correct. If correct, please book one extra bed for our 10-year-old son.

我已從您網站上看過住房規定。上面寫說兒童可以和父母同住一間房（可加床或不加床），且12歲以下的兒童是不會額外收費的。我想確認我對該規定的理解是否正確。如果無誤，我想幫同行的10歲兒子加一張床。

其他加床要求的相關問句：

1. Can you inform me of your hotel policies regarding children sharing rooms and extra bed requests?

   可否請您告知有關兒童同住一間房或加床的收費規定。

2. Are there extra charges for children under 7 years old?

   你們會針對7歲以下幼兒加床多收費用嗎？

3. Your hotel policies say that children above the age of 12 or adults will pay NT$800 per person, per night in an extra bed. Please confirm.

   你們住房規定上寫說12歲以上兒童或成人，每加一床每晚要多付800元。請確認。

主題4

Unit
06 生日派對

寫作策略 AB

Step **1** **Who** is the invitation for? 邀請誰？

Mr. and Mrs. Smith

Step **2** **Why** do you have the party? 慶祝什麼？

to celebrate my grandfather's 80th birthday

Step **3** **When** will the party be held? 什麼時候？

date, time

Step **4** **Where** is the party held? 地點在哪？

restaurant, address

Step **5** Ask to **Respond** 要求回覆

reply the email or make a call, deadline for response

Outline 這樣擬

破　題	宴會舉辦之時間／地點／目的。
邀　約	誠懇邀請對方出席，彰顯對方身分重要性。

懇請回覆　請對方確認是否出席，註明回覆方式以及截止時間。
期待出席　文末以一句短語再次力邀對方出席。
信　　尾　客套語＋署名。

 看看老師怎麼寫 🌐

Dear Mr. and Mrs. Smith,

We are planning to **throw a** dinner **party** to celebrate my grandfather's 80th birthday.

It'll be held next Friday, November 15th, from 7 p.m. to 10 p.m. at Wendy's Restaurant's. It's at No. 3, Section 3, Ming-Chuan East Road, Taipei City.

We would **be** very **pleased if** you could **attend** this party. It's an **informal gathering** and we only invited a few relatives and close friends. You have long been dear friends to our family, and we **sincerely** hope you can join us for this significant occasion.

Please respond to this email or call me by this Sunday to let me know if you can come, so we can make reservations and be well-prepared.

We **look forward to hearing** that you could be with us.

Sincerely yours,
Jennifer Chen

主題 4

親愛的史密絲夫婦：

我們正計畫為我祖父的八十大壽籌備晚宴。

時間為下週五，也就是十一月十五日，晚間七點到十點，在溫蒂餐廳，地址是台北市明川東路三段3號。

兩位若能蒞臨這場慶生會，我們將感到十分開心。這是個非正式的聚會，我們只邀請一些家族親友參加。兩位一向是我們家的密友，我們竭誠希望兩位可以蒞臨這個意義非凡的場合。

請您於這禮拜天之前以電子郵件或電話方式回覆，讓我知道兩位是否會出席，這樣我們才能預先訂位和準備。

我們竭誠期待您的大駕光臨。

Jennifer陳　敬上

關鍵單字片語

1. **throw a party** 辦派對 (= have a party = hold a party)
   Lisa is busy planning to throw a party for her new-born baby,
   Claire.
   Lisa正在為她剛出生的女兒Claire籌劃派對。

2. **attend**　v.　參加；出席 (= join = take part in = participate in)
   Jeremy Lin is going to attend a fund-raising cocktail party for
   charity.
   林書豪將會參加一場慈善募款雞尾酒會。

3. **informal**　adj.　非正式的 (同義：casual；反義：formal)
   I met my supervisor and had a joyful conversation at an
   informal occasion.
   我在一個非正式場合遇見我的主管，跟他相談甚歡。

4. **gathering**　n.　聚會 (= informal meeting, get-together)
   Bill is experienced in hosting social gatherings.
   Bill對於主持各種社交場合聚會很有經驗。

5. **sincerely**　adv.　竭誠；誠摯地 (= truly)
   We sincerely wish the earthquake-torn country could be back
   to its previous prosperity.
   我們竭誠盼望這個被地震重創的國家能恢復它之前的容景。

6. **Sincerely yours** 敬上 （書信結尾敬語，下一行接署名）

主題 4

給力句型解說 👉

人 be + adj. + if 條件子句
to V

I would be pleased if you can join us for dinner.

= I would be glad to have you for dinner.

如果你能加入我們的晚餐，我會很高興。

延伸句型：

pleased 感到開心的 honored 感到榮幸的 delighted 感到愉快的 grateful 感到感激的 glad 感到高興的		if you can honor us with your presence. to have your presence

人 + would be + | +

= It's my honor/pleasure/delight + if 子句 / to V

look forward to + N / V-ing

I look forward to your response.

我期待你的回覆。

I look forward to hearing from you soon.

我期待早日得到你的消息。

換個對象寫寫看

Dear **Mary**,

Next Monday is my birthday, and **I'm planning to celebrate my birthday with my close friends this Sunday afternoon. Let's get together for coffee, waffles, and honey toast at Honey Toast Café at 2:30 p.m**.

The honey toast there is the best in Town. But it's only great with you around.

Please call or text me by tomorrow to confirm your presence, so I can arrange seats.

You must come!

Kisses and hugs,

Judy Lin

親愛的**Mary**：

下週一是我生日，我打算這個禮拜天下午和我的好友一起慶祝。我們下午兩點半一起到蜜糖土司咖啡館喝咖啡、吃鬆餅和蜜糖土司吧！

她們家的蜜糖土司是全城最棒的，但再好的餐點沒有你在旁邊就沒意思了。

明天以前打電話或傳簡訊給我確認你會出席，這樣我才能處理訂位事宜。

你一定要來喔！

抱抱親親，

Judy 林

主題 4

好用句型大補湯 📋

邀約長官/上司

I have the pleasure in inviting you to attend this party. I have long been appreciative of your support at work, and it would be nice if you and your wife can honor us with your presence.

我很榮幸能邀約您參加這場派對。我一直以來都很感激您在工作上給予我的支持，若您與您的貴夫人能光臨，那就太好了。

邀約同事

I hope you can join us at this party. It won't be fun without you and your joyful conversation! Please do come so we can have fun together!

我很希望你可以參加這場派對。要是沒有你的妙語如珠，就不好玩了。一定要來喔，這樣我們才能一起盡情玩樂。

其他常用代換句：

1. We would be very delighted / pleased if you can come.
   如果你能參加，我們將會很高興。

2. We sincerely hope you will be able to attend.
   我們衷心希望您能出席。

3. I would appreciate if you could respond to this invitation by the end of this week.
   如果您能在本週末前回覆邀請，我將不勝感激。

4. Please kindly give me an answer by this Friday, so I can prepare well.
   請您能在本週五前回覆，以便讓我能妥善準備。

主題 4

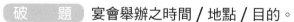

Unit
07 喬遷

寫作策略 AB

Step 1　**Who** are you writing to? 對象

Jeremy Lin

Step 2　**When** will the party be held? 什麼時候？

date, time

Step 3　**Where** will the party be held? 地點在哪？

address

Step 4　Ask to **Respond** 要求回覆

text or call, deadline for response

Outline 這樣擬

破　　題	宴會舉辦之時間 / 地點 / 目的。
邀　　約	誠懇邀請對方出席。
宴會細節	說明宴會主題/內容。
懇請回覆	請對方確認是否出席，註明回覆方式以及截止時間。
信　　尾	客套語＋署名。

看看老師怎麼寫

Dear Jeremy,

We're pleased to **inform** you that we've just moved in to our new apartment at Zhongxiao E. Rd.

Next Saturday, Mar 16th, 12 p.m., we'll have a house-warming party, and you and all the other colleagues are **cordially** invited to our apartment.

It's at 3F, No.3, Lane 20, Alley 55, Sec.3, Zhongxiao E. Rd. Da-An District, Taipei City.

We'll **have** the lunch, snacks, and cocktail **catered** on that day. So **all you need to do is** just **make yourself at home**, and enjoy the good food and music we prepare for you.

We really hope you can join us. We can't wait to **show** you **around**!
Please let us know by this Saturday if you'll come.

Affectionately,
Mr. and Mrs. Eric Lin

親愛的Jeremy：

通知你一個好消息，我們剛搬進了在忠孝東路的新公寓。

下禮拜六，三月十六號，中午十二點，我們會舉辦喬遷派對。竭誠邀請你和所有其他同事來我們家。

地址是台北市大安區忠孝東路三段55巷20弄3號3樓。

當天我會請外燴包辦午餐、點心、以及雞尾酒。所以你唯一要做的事就是把這兒當自己家，好好享受我們準備的美食和音樂。

我們真的希望你能加入。等不及要帶你看看我們的新家！
本週六前請讓我們知道你是否會出席。

你的好友，
Eric林 夫婦

關鍵單字片語

1. **inform** *v.* 通知 (= notify, tell)

   Please inform me of any changes you make regarding the proposal.

   你若對這個企劃案內容做任何改變，請通知我。

2. **cordially** *adv.* 誠摯地

   You are cordially invited to our wedding on Sept 18th.

   我們誠摯邀請你參加我們九月十八日的婚禮。

3. **cater** *v.* 承辦筵席 (+ for)

   This chef works in a restaurant and caters for weddings and parties.

   這位主廚在餐廳工作，也承辦婚禮和宴會的筵席。

4. **make oneself at home** 有如在自己家一樣放鬆享受

   The hostess told her guests, "Make yourselves at home and help yourselves to the snacks."

   女主人對她的賓客說：「把這兒當自己家，要吃點心就自己取用。」

5. **show someone around** 帶某人參觀環境

   The teacher asked the class leader to show his new classmate around the school.

   老師要求班長帶新同學參觀學校環境。

7. **affectionately** 充滿深情地 （用於書信結尾，下一行接署名)）

主題 4

給力句型解說 👉

人 + have + 事情 + p.p. 人請他人將事情辦好

I had the lunch catered. 我請人幫我承辦午餐筵席。

= I had the lunch catered (by some cooks).

使役動詞**have**的使用：

A請B處理某事

1. A + have + B + 原型動詞

2. A + have + 事情 + p.p. (by B)

I'll have the mechanic fix my car.

= I'll have my car fixed (by a mechanic).

我請技術人員修好我的車。

All you need/have to do is + (to) 原型動詞 你唯一要做的事情是…

All you need to do is wait for his call.

= All you need to do is to wait for his call.

你唯一要做的事就是等他的電話。

Dear **Neighbors**,
We've just moved in to this same building on the 13th floor. We're delighted to be neighbors with you.

Next Friday, Mar 15, at 7 p.m., we'll have a house-warming dinner party, and we'd like to invite everyone in this building to share our joys.

As for the dinner, please bring a dish to the party, so everyone can share. It'll be a great chance for all the neighbors to enjoy dinner and get to know one another.

Please let me know by next Monday if you'll come.

Your new neighbors,
Mr. and Mrs. Joseph Chang

親愛的鄰居們：
我們剛搬入本棟大樓的13樓。很開心和你們成為鄰居。
下週五，三月十五號，晚上七點，我們會舉辦喬遷晚宴，想邀請本棟大樓所有鄰居來參加。
至於晚餐，請帶一道菜來，這樣一來大家就能一同分享。這是個讓鄰居們好好享受晚餐並彼此認識的好機會。
請在下週一前讓我知道您是否會出席。

您的新鄰居，
Joseph Chang夫婦

主題4

好用句型大補湯

邀約長官/上司

The honor will be mine if you can find the time to attend the party. I have also invited all the colleagues to join us. It means a lot to me if we can all get together and have fun.

若您能參加這場派對，那將是我莫大的榮幸。我也已邀請所有同事加入。若大家能一起同歡，對我來說意義非凡。

邀約好友

I'm more than glad to invite you to my new home.　With you, the fun will double up!

我超興奮要邀請你來我的新家。有你在身旁，歡樂會倍增！

喬遷邀請卡片其他寫法：

1. Mr. and Mrs. Eric Lin request the honor of your presence at our Housewarming.

   Eric林夫婦希望有這個榮幸可以請您出席喬遷派對。

2. Mr. and Mrs. Eric Lin cordially invite you to a lunch to celebrate the completion of our new home.

   Eric林夫婦竭誠邀請您出席午餐派對，一同慶祝新居落成。

3. Please join us in celebration of our new home.

請加入我們一起慶祝新居喬遷之喜。

4. Construction is complete! Please join us in celebration of our new home.

新居落成！請加入我們一起慶祝新居喬遷之喜。

MEMO

Unit

08 婚禮

寫作策略 AB

Step **1** **Who** are you writing to? 對象

Helen and David

Step **2** **When** will the ceremony be held? 什麼時候？

date, time

Step **3** **Where** is the wedding held? 地點在哪？

Garden Hotel

Step **4** Ask to **Respond** 要求回覆

call, deadline for response

Outline 這樣擬

破　　題	婚宴舉辦之時間／地點
邀　　約	誠懇邀請對方出席。
宴會細節	說明婚宴主題／內容。
懇請回覆	請對方確認是否出席，註明回覆方式以及截止時間。
信　　尾	客套語＋署名。

看看老師怎麼寫

Dear Helen and David,

Julian and I are getting married! It is with great pleasure that I invite you to the **wedding** on Saturday, May 18th at Garden Hotel at No. 10 Sec. 5,　Zhongxiao East Road Xinyi District, Taipei.

We are asking all our relatives and friends to be present, and would be very glad to have you among them.

This outdoor ceremony will **take place** at four o'clock at the garden **with** a live band **playing** songs. Afterwards, there will be an informal **reception**.

RSVP with the **attached** card by next Friday April 14th.

I wish you would all **be able to** join this special occasion.

With kindest **regards**, I am
Sincerely yours,
Juliet Huang

主題 4

親愛的Helen和David：

Julian和我要結婚了！我很榮幸想邀請您參加我們的婚禮。時間是五月十八日星期六，地點在Garden Hotel，地址是台北市信義區忠孝東路五段十號。

我們正在邀請所有親友出席，很開心您也在受邀之列。

這場戶外婚禮會在下午四點在戶外花園舉行，同時有現場樂團演奏歌曲，讓所有賓客都可以享受空氣中瀰漫的花香和音樂。

附上一封回函。請您下週五，四月十四號之前回覆。

我希望您們都能來參加這別具意義的聚會。

獻上我最深的祝福
Juliet Huang敬上

關鍵單字片語

1. **wedding** *n.* 婚禮

   The couple will invite all their colleagues to their wedding.

   這對新人會邀請他們所有同事參加他們的婚禮。

2. **reception** *n.* 筵席；招待宴會

   Our public relations department is arranging the reception dinner.

   我們的公關部門正在籌備這場接待晚宴。

3. **take place** 舉辦；發生 (= be held, be hosted, occur)

   This accident took place two years ago.

   這場意外發生在兩年前。

4. **RSVP**敬請回覆（請帖用語），法文：répondez s'il vous plaît

5. **attached** *adj.* 附上 (=enclosed)

   Attached please find my resume and a recommendation letter.

   附件請看我的履歷表以及一封推薦信。

6. **regards** *n.* 問候；致意（一定要用複數型）

   Please give my regards to your parents.

   請代我問候您的父母。

主題 4

給力句型解說 👉

with +名詞 +	Adj. V-ing (表主動) p.p. (表被動)	+ 附加說明名詞的狀態

1. He eats with his mouth open. 他吃東西時嘴巴張開。

   = He eats while his mouth is open.

   （形容詞open形容名詞mouth的狀態）

2. He eats with his mouth watering. 他吃東西時一邊流口水。

   = He eats and his mouth waters.

   （主動語態動詞water，改成V-ing形容名詞mouth的狀態）

3. He eats with his mouth shut. 他吃東西時嘴巴閉著。

   = He eats and his mouth is shut.

   （被動語態動詞is shut，保留p.p.形容名詞mouth的狀態）

be able to V = have the ability to V. = can + 原型動詞 = be capable of + V-ing 能夠去做…

He is able to swim 40 meters without breathing.

= He has the ability to swim 40 meters without breathing.

= He can swim 40 meters without breathing.

= He is capable of swimming 40 meters without breathing.

他能夠游40公尺不換氣。

換個對象寫寫看

Dear **Janet**,

My fiancée Alice and I are getting married! You are cordially invited to our wedding on Sunday, May 19th at Ball Room, M Hotel at 9 Sec. 2, Hoping West Road Xinyi District, Taipei.

We are asking all our intimate colleagues to be present, and would be very glad to have you among them.

This ceremony will take place at 11 o'clock with DJs playing music. Afterwards there will be a reception lunch.

RSVP with the attached card by next Monday April 11th.

I wish you would all be able to join this special occasion.

Sincerely yours,

Tony Fan

親愛的**Janet**：

我和我的未婚妻**Alice**要結婚了！誠邀您參加我們的婚禮。時間是五月十九日星期日，地點在**M Hotel**，地址是台北市信義區和平西路二段九號。

我們正在邀請所有熟識的同事出席，很開心您也在受邀之列。

這場婚禮會在下午四點舉行，同時有DJ播放歌曲，之後會有午餐筵席。

附上一封回函。請您在下週一四月十一號之前回覆。

我希望你們都能來參加這別具意義的聚會。

Tony Fan敬上

主題4

好用句型大補湯

邀約長官/上司參加自己的兒女的婚禮

Jenny and I would like to request the pleasure of your company in joining us to celebrate the marriage of our son Grandson and his fiancée Debbie.

Jenny和我誠邀您賞光參與，一同慶賀我的兒子Grandson和他的未婚妻Debbie的婚禮。

邀約好友參加自己的婚禮

It's the most important day in my life, and I hope I can have you around. Please come!

這是我生命中最重要的一天，我希望有我的好友相伴。你一定要來！

回覆婚宴邀請的書寫參考：

1. 可出席：

Mr. and Mrs. David Lin accept with pleasure Mr. and Mrs. Henry Huang's kind invitation to be present at the marriage of their daughter Juliet Huang to Mr. Julian Kao on Friday, the sixteenth of May at four o'clock and afterward at the reception dinner.

David Lin夫婦欣喜接受Henry Huang夫婦的邀請，出席他們的女兒Juliet Huang和Julian Kao在五月十六日下午四點舉辦的的婚禮，以及之後的晚宴。

2. 無法出席：

Mr. and Mrs. David Lin exceedingly regret that they are unable to accept Mr. and Mrs. Henry Huang's kind invitation to be present at the marriage of their daughter Juliet Huang to Mr. Julian Kao on Friday, the sixteenth of May at four o'clock and afterward at the reception dinner.

David Lin夫婦萬分遺憾無法出席Henry Huang夫婦的女兒Juliet Huang和Julian Kao在五月十六日下午四點舉辦的的婚禮，以及之後的晚宴。

MEMO

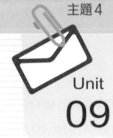

Unit 09 感謝老師推薦函

寫作策略

Step 1　**Who** is the Thank-you Card for? 寫給誰？
Prof. Michelle Lee

Step 2　**Why** do you thank him/her for? 感謝什麼？
writing a letter of recommendation

Step 3　**How** does that affect you? 影響你什麼？
priority

Outline 這樣擬

破　　題　寫感謝信的目的（對方做了什麼讓你感恩在心）
影　　響　對方的恩惠帶給你的影響。
再次致謝
信　　尾　客套語＋署名。

看看老師怎麼寫

Dear Prof. Lee,

I can't thank you enough for the letters of recommendation you wrote for my job applications.

I know you put a lot of time and effort into them. Your endorsement surely gives me an edge over other applicants. I hope you know how much I appreciate it.

I will keep you posted on any responses I get.

Thanks again with gratitude!

Sincerely,

Oscar Hong

中文翻譯

親愛的李教授：

您幫我寫的求職推薦信，讓我萬分感謝。

我知道您花了很多時間和心力在寫這些推薦信。您的背書確實讓我比其他的求職者更有優勢。我希望您知道我有多麼感激您。

若我有收到任何求職的回覆，我會隨時讓您知道。

再次以感恩的心向您致謝。

Oscar 洪　敬上

主題 4

關鍵單字片語

1. **recommendation** *n.* 推薦

   I need to get letters of recommendation from my boss or supervisors in my previous company.

   我需要向我之前工作的公司老闆或主管索取推薦信。

2. **application** *n.* 申請；應徵

   The university welcomes applications from both native and overseas students.

   這所大學歡迎本國或海外學生申請。

3. **effort** *n.* 努力

   It takes a lot of time and effort to get an exhibition ready.

   要辦好一場展覽需要很多時間和心力。

4. **endorsement** *n.* 背書

   Celebrity endorsements are widely used as a way to promote products.

   名人背書或代言是普遍常用的產品宣傳手法。

5. **an edge over ...** 比⋯更有優勢

   The next version of the smart phone will have the edge over its competitors.

   這個智慧型手機的新版本會讓它比其他競爭者更有優勢。

6. **keep sb. posted** 隨時告知某人最新訊息

   I'll keep you posted on the progress of the election.

   我會隨時告訴你選舉的進展。

給力句型解說

疑問詞 + S + V 疑問詞引導的名詞子句（作為動詞的受詞）

I hope you know how much I appreciate your efforts.

我希望您知道我有多麼感激您的付出。

名詞子句：「可以當名詞的句子」，可作為句子裡的主詞或受詞。

1. **that + S + V**（常作為主要子句動詞的受詞，**that**可被省略）

   I believe (that) he will come to our party.

   我相信他一定會來參加我們的派對。

2. **疑問詞 + S + V**（常見的間接問句類型）

   直接問句：What time is it?

   間接問句：Can you tell me what time it is.

   　　　　　現在幾點？

keep + N. + 補語（adj. / p.p. /V-ing）讓N.保持…的狀態

I will keep you posted/informed when I get any responses.

→ 用**p.p. (posted/informed)** 描述受詞**you**。

我若有得到任何回應，會隨時告知你。

Please keep the door open/closed at all times.

→ 用**adj. (open)**或**p.p. (closed)** 描述受詞**the door**。

請讓此門保持開啟/關閉狀態。

They offer good service to keep their customers coming.

→ 用**V-ing (coming)** 描述受詞**their customers**。

她們提供好服務讓顧客不斷上門。

換個對象寫寫看

Dear **Prof. Sandy Chen**,

I want to express my gratitude for the letters of recommendation you wrote for my applications to graduate schools.

I know you put a lot of time and effort into them. **Your recommendation really helps a lot. I can't thank you enough and will be forever grateful.**

I will keep you posted on any responses I get.

Thanks again!

Sincerely,

Benjamin Tsai

親愛的陳教授：

我想要表達我對您的謝意，感謝您為我撰寫申請研究所的推薦信。

我知道您花了很多時間和心力在寫這些推薦信。您的推薦對我幫助很大。我萬分感謝，也將永遠感激您。

若我有收到任何學校的回覆，我會隨時讓您知道。

再次向您致謝。

Benjamin蔡　敬上

好用句型大補湯

感謝對方指導碩士論文／研究

I wish to express my sincere gratitude for your supervision and guidance. Your assistance has led me to complete my master thesis. I wish you well and hope that I will make you proud.

我想要表達我誠摯的感謝，感謝您的監督與指導。您的協助引領我完成碩士論文。敬祝您一切平安，也希望我能讓你引以為傲。

感謝對方教學上的付出

I just wanted to let you know how much I appreciate everything you've done to improve my reading skills. You've helped build the foundation for reading and improved my academic performance. The impact of your help is so significant. I truly can't thank you enough and will be forever grateful.

我只想讓您知道我有多麼感激您為了增進我的閱讀技巧所做的一切。您幫我奠定了閱讀的基礎，也提升了我的學業表現。您的幫助對我的影響甚鉅。我再怎麼感激也不為過，我會永遠感恩您。

其他萬用謝師語：

1. Thank you for teaching such a great class for the past few years. I have learned a lot from you.
   謝謝你這幾年來精采的授課。我在您身上學到很多。
2. Thanks for always being patient and enthusiastic. I always looked forward to attending your class.
   謝謝您總是很有耐心和熱情。我總是期待上您的課。
3. I want to thank you for being such a fantastic teacher. I had a terrific experience in your class.
   我想說聲「謝謝您」，您是一位很棒的老師。您的課堂讓我如沐春風。

主題 4

Unit
10
感謝寄宿家庭照料

寫作策略 ᴬᴮ

Step **1** **Who** is the Thank-you Card for? 寫給誰？
Mr. and Mrs. Davis

Step **2** **Why** do you thank him/her for? 感謝什麼？
for their hospitality

Step **3** **How** will you return the favor? 怎麼回報？
invite them over

Outline 這樣擬

破　　題　寫感謝信的目的。
詳述對方恩情　具體說明對方提供的恩惠。
再次致謝　除了致謝外，也可以表達你想要回報的意圖。
信　　尾　客套語＋署名。

看看老師怎麼寫 🌐

My dearest Mr. and Mrs. Davis,
Thank you for your hospitality during my stay in Canada.

I learned a lot about Vancouver because you took me to many places. It was my first homestay and first time abroad, so I was a little nervous. However, your family was very kind, so I enjoyed it very much. I had a great time during the trip and I came back to Taiwan with a lot of good memories.
I'll send an email to you and send letters with photos. Please come visit me in Taiwan someday if you can. I'll show you around. Keep in touch!

With love,
Amy Lai

中文翻譯 📝

親愛的Davis夫婦：
謝謝你們的盛情款待，讓我在加拿大期間寄宿在你們家。

因為你們帶我逛很多地方，讓我多認識溫哥華。這是我第一次待在寄宿家庭，也是我第一次出國，所以我有點緊張。但你們一家人很親切，所以我玩得很盡興，帶著很多美好的回憶回到台灣。
我會寄email和附有照片的信件給你們。如果可以的話，歡迎你們來台灣找我玩。我會帶你們四處走走。

我們保持聯絡。

愛你們的，
Amy 賴

關鍵單字片語

1. **hospitality** *n.* 熱情

   Many foreign tourists are impressed with the hospitality of the people in Taiwan.

   很多國外旅客對於台灣人的熱情印象深刻。

2. **homestay** *n.* 寄宿家庭

   I sent a thank-you note to my homestay family in America for their kindness.

   我寄了一張感謝卡給我在美國的寄宿家庭，感謝他們的照顧。

3. **abroad** *adv.* 在國外 (= overseas)

   The top student got a scholarship to support him to study abroad.

   這位頂尖學生拿到獎學金以資助他在國外求學。

4. **however** *adv.* 然而 (= nevertheless, but)

   He stayed up late to prepare for the final exam. However, he failed.

   他熬夜準備期末考，但他考不及格。

5. **have a great time** 玩得很盡興 (= have fun = enjoy oneself)

   A: How was your trip to Ilan? B: It was fun! I really had a great time.

   A: 你的宜蘭之旅過得如何？ B: 很好玩。我玩得很開心。

6. **memory**　*n.*　記憶

He has lots of happy memories of his stay in Japan.

他待在日本期間留下很多快樂的回憶。

給力句型解說

a little + 形容詞 / 副詞 / 介系詞片語　有一點…

You seem a little **annoyed** by her harsh remarks.

你似乎有點被她的嚴厲批評激怒了。

He takes it a little **too seriously**.

他把事情看的有點嚴重。

I'm a little **under the weather these days**.

我這幾天有一點身體不適。

S + V + very much　很…

I appreciate your effort very much.

我很感謝你付出的心力。

very 和 **very much** 用法大不同：

1. **very + 形容詞 / 副詞**

   That actor is very famous.

   那位演員很帥。

   He works very hard.

   他工作得很認真。

2. **very much 放在動詞的後面**

   We admire him very much.

   我們很崇拜他。

主題 4

換個對象寫寫看

Dear **Allen and Crystal**,

Thank you for the amazing dinner party at your house last Friday.

The food was fabulous and those wines were outstanding. Everything was delicious, including of course that exquisite dessert you made. And that card game was a riot. I am still laughing thinking about it.

It was so nice to finally catch up. I look forward to more fun in the future!

Thank you again for your hospitality.

Warm regards,
Teddy and Karen

親愛的**Allen和Crystal**：

謝謝你們邀請我參加上週五在你們家舉辦的晚宴。

晚宴上食物很美味，美酒也是一絕。每樣食物都很可口，也包含了你們親手烘焙的精緻甜點。而且撲克牌遊戲讓氣氛變得很熱絡。我現在想到還會會心一笑。

很開心終於有時間聚會聊聊。期待未來再找時間一起同樂。

再次謝謝你們的熱情款待。

Teddy 和Karen 致意

好用句型大補湯

感謝國外室友對自己的照顧和陪伴

Thank you so much for your companionship and all your kindness while I was in Canada. I will never forget the jokes we shared, and I miss your hand-made cookies.

在我待在加拿大這段期間，感謝你的陪伴和你的關照。我永遠不會忘記我們共同分享的笑語，也很想念你的手工餅乾。

感謝國外同學對自己的幫忙和協助

I'd like to thank you for your generous help with both my schoolwork and personal life. Thank you for showing me around the campus on my first day of school, and giving me a lift home from time to time.

我想感謝你在學業和生活上給我的慷慨協助！謝謝你在我上學第一天帶我參觀認識校園，也謝謝你三不五時開車順帶載我回家。

其他萬用感謝語：

1. Thank you for your warm hospitality. We felt as comfortable as in our own home.
   謝謝你的熱情接待，讓我們倍感賓至如歸。
2. I wish to express my earnest gratitude for all your kindness.
   感謝您給我的協助，我將永遠銘記在心。
3. Thank you so much from the bottom of my heart.
   我由衷感謝您。

主題4

Unit
11

感謝貼心服務

寫作策略

Step **1** **Who** is the Thank-you Card for? 寫給誰？

Mr. William Chou

Step **2** **Why** do you thank him/her for? 感謝什麼？

for providing useful information on touring the city

Step **3** **How** will you return the favor? 怎麼回報？

will visit again

Outline 這樣擬

破　　題	寫感謝信的原因
詳　　述	說明對方提供的服務，令你留下深刻印象。
再次致謝	表達你將回報（會推薦親友來訪或會再度來訪）。
信　　尾	客套語＋署名。

看看老師怎麼寫

Dear Mr. Chou,

I just wanted to thank you for your excellent and friendly services you provided during our stay at the Ritz.

We really enjoyed our honeymoon at your hotel. The suite overlooking the river had a breath-taking view. The room service was also unmatched; and your housekeeping staff was really professional. And I'd like to thank you for the useful information you provided on touring the city.

I am very impressed with your high-quality service and will definitely recommend the Ritz to other people.

Thank you again for an exceptional service and hospitality.

Wishing you all the best,
Stephan and Cindy Huang

主題4

親愛的周先生：

我只是想感謝麗池酒店在我下榻這段期間所提供的高品質又親切的服務。

我們在貴酒店下榻度蜜月，十分愉快。我們的套房眺望河景，視野美得令人忘了呼吸。客房服務也無與倫比，你們的清潔人員十分專業。我也想謝謝您提供我們有用的旅遊資訊。

你們高品質的服務讓我留下深刻的印象。我一定會推薦其他人來下榻麗池酒店。

再次謝謝你們獨一無二的服務與款待。

祝你們全體人員萬事如意。

Stephan and Cindy

關鍵單字片語

1. **service** *n.* 服務

   The aim of this hotel is to provide the best service at the lowest price.

   這間飯店的目標是以最低的價格提供最棒的服務。

2. **honeymoon** *n.* 蜜月

   This newly-wed couple went to Italy for their honeymoon.

   這對新婚夫婦去義大利度蜜月。

3. **suite** *n.* 套房

   The rock star is treated to stay one night at the presidential suite.

   這位搖滾巨星被招待免費在總統套房住一晚。

4. **overlook** *v.* 眺望

   Our room overlooks the ocean, and we can see the lighthouse in the distance.

   我們的房間可眺望海景，且可以看到遠方的燈塔。

5. **housekeeping** *n.* 清理房間

   This company is in charge of the catering and housekeeping at the hotel.

   這間公司負責這家飯店的餐飲外燴和客房清潔服務。

6. **professional** *adj.* 專業的

   This business campaign looks very professional.

   這個商業宣傳活動看起來很專業。

主題4

給力句型解說 👆

現在分詞 V-ing當形容詞的用法

1. **情緒動詞V-ing** 表示「令人感到...的」，多半形容事、物。

   The suite has a breath-taking view.

   這間套房有令人秉氣凝神的美景。

2. **一般動詞V-ing**形容名詞的「性質、功用」或「正在做⋯」。

   He works in an advertising company.　他在一家廣告公司上班。

   →advertising描述company的「性質」。

   Be careful of the boiling water. 小心這正在滾沸的水。

   →boiling描述water「正在」滾沸中。

3. **關係子句中，省略關係詞which/who/that**，後面「主動語態」動詞轉變成V-ing。

   The suite **which overlooks** the river has a perfect view.

   = The suite **overlooking** the river has a perfect view.

   這個眺望河景的套房擁有絕佳視野。

4. **分詞構句中，省略重複的主詞**，後面「主動語態」動詞轉變成V-ing。

   Because this suite overlooks the river, it offers perfect view.

   = Overlooking the river, the hotel offers perfect view.

過去分詞 p.p.當形容詞的用法

1. **情緒動詞p.p.** 表示「感到...的」，形容人的情緒。

   The heart-broken girl cried day and night.

   這個心碎的女孩日夜都在哭泣。

2. **一般動詞p.p.**形容名詞「被⋯⋯」或「已經⋯⋯」。

   He cried over the broken vase. 他為了這只被打破的花瓶哭泣。

→broken描述vase「被」打破。

I only drink boiled water. 我只喝已經煮開的水。

→boiled描述water「已經」煮過了。

3. 關係子句中，省略關係詞which/who/that，後面「被動語態」動詞只保留p.p.。

The hotel **which is located** downtown has convenient transportation

= The hotel **located** downtown has convenient transportation.

這家位於市中心的旅館提供便利的交通。

4. 分詞構句中，省略重複的主詞，後面「被動語態」動詞只保留p.p.。

Because this hotel is situated near the airport, it offers great transportation.

= Situated near the airport, this hotel offers great transportation.

因為這家旅館鄰近機場，交通便利。

主題 4

換個對象寫寫看

Dear **Ms. Gore**,

Claire and I just wanted to thank you for touching services you provided during our stay at the Ritz.

We really enjoyed our stay at your hotel. On top of that, we were very impressed with your help with any of our requests. Thank you for getting dinner reservations, and for last minute theater tickets. You even assisted booking tours and organizing a shopping journey for my family.

Thank you again for an exceptional service. We will definitely recommend the Ritz to other people.

Wish you all the best,
Sean and Claire Wang

親愛的**Ms. Gore**：

Claire和我想感謝在我們下榻這麗池酒店這段期間您所提供的貼心服務。

我們在貴酒店度過歡樂時光。更重要的是，您努力協助我們各項需求，讓我們留下深刻印象，謝謝你幫我們預約到餐廳吃晚餐，也趕在電影開演前一刻幫我們拿到票。您甚至還幫我們一家預定觀光行程以及安排購物之旅。

再次謝謝你們獨一無二的服務與款待。我一定會推薦其他人來下榻麗池酒店。

祝你們全體人員萬事如意。

Sean 和 Claire王

好用句型大補湯

感謝服務人員協助洗燙衣服，以及處理文書雜務

I am writing to thank you for the very high standard of laundry service you provided. And we were touched with your assistance with secretarial services, such as faxing and copying documents. Your high-quality services for business customers are unparalleled!

我想感謝你們提供高標準的洗衣服務。你們協助我們處理行政秘書工作（例如傳真與影印等）也令人倍感窩心。你們為商務旅客提供的高品質服務無與倫比！

給飯店服務人員的小費：

Bellman/Porte搬運行李人員：一件行李最少2美金
Concierge櫃檯服務人員：5-20美金（依服務內容而訂，特別貼心服務可給高達20美金小費）
Housekeeper房間清潔人員：一晚2-5美金，每日支付
Parking Valet泊車小弟：取車時給2-5美金
Room service客房服務：5美金（除非小費已內含在結帳金額裡）

主題 4

Leader 034

一本就能 Hold 住工作、享受生活的情境英語 Email 寫作書

附超值便利貼光碟,輕鬆寫信!

作　　者	力得編輯群
發 行 人	周瑞德
執行總監	齊心瑀
執行編輯	魏于婷
校　　對	編輯部
封面構成	高鍾琪

內頁構成	華漢電腦排版有限公司
印　　製	大亞彩色印刷製版股份有限公司
初　　版	2016 年 1 月
定　　價	新台幣 349 元
出　　版	力得文化
電　　話	(02) 2351-2007
傳　　真	(02) 2351-0887
地　　址	100 台北市中正區福州街 1 號 10 樓之 2
E - m a i l	best.books.service@gmail.com
網　　址	www.bestbookstw.com

港澳地區總經銷	泛華發行代理有限公司
地　　址	香港新界將軍澳工業邨駿昌街 7 號 2 樓
電　　話	(852) 2798-2323
傳　　真	(852) 2796-5471

國家圖書館出版品預行編目資料

一本就能 Hold 住工作、享受生活的情境英語 Email 寫作
書 / 力得編輯群著. -- 初版. -- 臺北市 : 力得文化,
2016.01
　面 ；　公分. -- (Leader ; 34)
ISBN 978-986-92398-3-7(平裝附光碟片)

1.英語 2.電子郵件 3.應用文

805.179　104027779